EXPELLED

JIMMY PATTERSON BOOKS FOR YOUNG ADULT READERS

For exclusives, trailers, and other information, visit jamespatterson.com.

EXPELLED

JAMES PATTERSON

AND EMILY RAYMOND

JIMMY Patterson Books
LITTLE, BROWN AND COMPANY
NEW YORK BOSTON LONDON

Hachette Book Group supports the right to free expression and the value of copyright. The purpose of copyright is to encourage writers and artists to produce the creative works that enrich our culture.

The scanning, uploading, and distribution of this book without permission is a theft of the author's intellectual property. If you would like permission to use material from the book (other than for review purposes), please contact permissions@hbgusa.com. Thank you for your support of the author's rights.

JIMMY Patterson Books / Little, Brown and Company
Hachette Book Group
1290 Avenue of the Americas, New York, NY 10104
jimmypatterson.org

First Edition: October 2017

JIMMY Patterson Books is an imprint of Little, Brown and Company, a division of Hachette Book Group, Inc. The Little, Brown name and logo are trademarks of Hachette Book Group, Inc. The JIMMY Patterson Books® name and logo are trademarks of JBP Business, LLC.

The publisher is not responsible for websites (or their content) that are not owned by the publisher.

The Hachette Speakers Bureau provides a wide range of authors for speaking events. To find out more, go to hachettespeakersbureau.com or call (866) 376-6591.

"Wild Geese" from *Dream Work* by Mary Oliver. Copyright © 1986 by Mary Oliver. Used by permission of Grove Atlantic, Inc. Excerpt from "This Be the Verse" from *The Complete Poems of Philip Larkin* by Philip Larkin, edited by Archie Burnett. Copyright © 2012 by The Estate of Philip Larkin. Reprinted by permission of Farrar, Straus and Giroux.

Library of Congress Cataloging-in-Publication Data
Names: Patterson, James, author. | Raymond, Emily, author.
Title: Expelled / James Patterson with Emily Raymond.
Description: First edition. | New York : JIMMY Patterson Books / Little, Brown and Company, 2017.
Summary: Expelled over the photo that was posted to his Twitter account, Theo Foster, seventeen, is determined to find out who took the picture and why he and three other students were targeted.
Identifiers: LCCN 2017009677 | ISBN 978-0-316-44039-4 (hc)
Subjects: | CYAC: Social media—Fiction. | Documentary films—Production and direction—Fiction. | High schools—Fiction. | Schools—Fiction. | Family problems—Fiction. | Grief—Fiction. | Mystery and detective stories.
Classification: LCC PZ7.P27653 Exp 2017 | DDC [Fic]—dc23
LC record available at https://lccn.loc.gov/2017009677

10 9 8 7 6 5 4 3 2 1

LSC-W

Printed in the United States of America

EXPELLED

I honestly don't know how I got here.

I understand, of course, that actions have consequences, and that *bad* actions have *bad* consequences (thank you, Principal Dekum, for that pearl of wisdom). But I'm still unclear on the chain of events that have landed me, Theo Foster—B+ student, school newspaper editor, bookish but essentially normal eleventh grader—at my own high school expulsion hearing.

I'm wearing a tie for the second time in my life, and my armpits are drenched with sweat. The room is hot, it smells like six different kinds of BO, and there's a panel of Pinewood School District board members shooting eye-daggers at me like I'm some perp in a low-budget episode of *Judge Judy*.

The hearing officer—a small, round man in a too-tight suit—clears his throat. "We are now in executive session," he announces, "and the matter at hand is the behavior of student Theodore James Foster. The Arlington High School administration recommends his expulsion for the remainder of the school year, for the offense of *educational disruption*. It will be up to the board to determine if this is appropriate disciplinary action."

I can't help it—I glance at the empty seat next to me.

"Are you expecting someone, Mr. Foster?" the hearing officer asks.

I've heard that some kids show up to expulsion hearings with lawyers. Probably, at the very least, they bring a pissed-off parent or two.

"My mom's at work," I say.

"And your father?" the hearing officer asks.

"I'm sure he'd love to be here," I answer, and though I know I should stop there, I don't. "The problem is that he's dead, so I don't think he's going to make it."

"Mr. Foster passed away ten months ago," Mr. Palmieri, the assistant principal, informs the hearing officer.

I hate the euphemism *pass away*—it sounds like a square dance move from middle school gym class. *Do-si-do your partner now, and pass away on down the row!* Incidentally, I also hate dancing.

"Regrets," the hearing officer offers in a monotone. "I will now ask the administration to read the charges and present information regarding the incident in question. A copy will be sent to Mrs. Foster for her signature."

Palmieri pops right up, salivating at his moment in the spotlight. If I'd thought mentioning my dead father would get me a shred of sympathy from anyone in this room, I was wrong.

"Theo Foster is the creator of a secret Twitter account that has been the source of gossip, rumor, and innuendo," Palmieri reads. "Although school administrators did not approve of his immature posts"—*Objection,* I feel like crying, *mischaracterization!*—"we did not pursue disciplinary action until he maliciously posted a photograph that permanently tarnished the reputation of a star athlete and our entire high school community."

The board members nod grimly. They'd have to live underground not to know what Palmieri's talking about. And though a couple of them do look grubby and subterrestrial, I'm pretty sure they live in houses and have access to the nightly news.

Then Palmieri pulls out Exhibit A: the picture I supposedly posted, which he's blown up and mounted on poster board. It's such an incredible photograph that I almost wish I *had* posted it—or, better yet, had been there when it happened.

The snap was taken at night about a week ago, in the grassy area between the school parking lot and the football field, right near the ARLINGTON HIGH SCHOOL, HOME OF THE FIGHTING TIGERS sign. In the foreground is Parker Harris, our star quarterback, drunk and shirtless. His chiseled pecs practically glow in the light of the flash. He's got a bottle of Jack Daniels in his right hand and the bare breasts of an unidentified female in *very* close proximity to his left. The girl is mid-twirl, so her swinging hair covers her face (her identity, naturally, has been the source of relentless speculation). Behind the happy twosome, someone wearing the big tiger head of our school mascot is captured, midstream, peeing on something that looks a *lot* like Parker's number 89 football jersey.

In other words, the picture is the platonic ideal of teen debauchery, and it's still being talked about on every TV station in the state so aging anchors can use it as proof of a "recent but steep decline in adolescent morality and values."

I can't help it; a tiny smile flickers across my face. I never liked Parker Harris, and I'd pay good money to know who took the picture.

But I'd also like to kick the ass of whoever's trying to make me take the fall for it.

Palmieri slaps the table in front of him. "This is no laughing matter, Mr. Foster," he yells. "What is wrong with you?"

That, honestly, is a question that'd take several hours to answer.

"I'm sorry, sir," I mumble.

"Do you have anything to say in your defense?"

"I didn't post the picture," I say, earnestly now. "I know it's my account, but I didn't post it."

Palmieri's eyes narrow. "Does anyone else have the password to the account?"

"No, but it's not that hard to figure out someone's—"

"Do you have an enemy, Mr. Foster, who would post something to your account? Is that what you're suggesting?"

We stare at each other. *My only enemy's you.* I shake my head no.

"You posted the picture, assuming you could claim innocence," Palmieri says.

"The IP address," I say. "Did you check it? That'll prove the post didn't come from me!"

Palmieri shakes his head. "Actually, Mr. Foster, all your posts originate from the same IP address. The picture was uploaded from your computer."

I'm stunned. I wasn't prepared for this, and I have no idea how it could have happened.

I look first at Palmieri and then at the glowering members of the school board. They don't know me at all, but it's obvious they've already judged me. It all becomes clear: there's no one on my side and no way of getting out of this mess. I don't know why I bothered with the stupid tie.

"I didn't post the picture," I repeat.

Palmieri shakes his head, like I've disappointed him yet again. "In the words of Robert Louis Stevenson, 'Everybody, sooner or later, sits down to a banquet of consequences.' I hope you are prepared for yours, Theo Foster."

The school board robots debate for approximately forty-five seconds before they come back with their decree: I'm expelled, forbidden to attend school or set foot on school property for the final three weeks of the school year.

And that's how quickly it happens: I go from promising junior to up-and-coming deadbeat.

Happy birthday to me.

2

A *belated wave of shock nearly* doubles me over in the hallway. I'm leaning against the wall, trying not to hyperventilate, when I hear someone call my name.

I look up. If the wall weren't keeping me vertical, I might've collapsed.

Sasha Ellis—*the* Sasha Ellis—is *also* at school district headquarters on a Thursday night. More importantly, Sasha Ellis is talking to me.

Sasha's in my homeroom, but she talks to no one. When she glides through school, eyes straight ahead and earbuds in deep, kids make way for her, just like minnows do for sharks. It's not that Sasha doesn't *like* anyone else—I don't think—it's more like she barely notices they exist.

Sasha pushes her dark hair out of her face and gazes at me with glacial blue eyes. She'd be incontestably beautiful if she didn't always look like she was on the verge of a scorn-induced migraine, but the sneer takes her down to a 9, tops.

"What are you doing here?" I manage.

She ignores the question, and *everybody* knows why I'm here. "I saw the picture. It's amazing."

"That's one way of describing it," I say. "Considering it just ruined my life."

"Seriously, it's like a Dash Snow polaroid or something."

"A what?"

Sasha rolls her eyes at my ignorance. She's crazy smart and possibly crazy, and—full disclosure—I have basically loved her for three years straight without her ever saying a word to me before this very second.

Well, love is maybe an overstatement. But the feeling is stronger than like and more complicated than lust, and so far I haven't figured out the perfect word for it.

"Whatever," I say. "You don't have to explain your references to me."

"He was this totally wild artist in New York. When he was, like, our age, he stole a Polaroid camera, and then he started taking all these insane party pictures, mostly so he could remember where he'd been the night before."

"Did he ever get anyone expelled?" I ask bitterly.

She ignores this question, too. "He was pretty famous," she says.

"What happened to him?"

"Let's just say it didn't end well."

I'm fine to drop the subject. "Okay. Seriously, though, why are you here?"

"Those are my tits in the picture," she says.

My mouth falls open.

"Just kidding," she says.

"But you and Parker—"

"Are nothing," she says. "That was almost three years ago."

In our freshman year, before she stopped talking to anyone, Sasha wore short bright dresses and kept her toenails painted like tiny pink shells. And, yeah, she dated Parker for a while. Most of the Arlington girls have, but Sasha was the first. People say he still loves her, but personally I doubt he is capable of such emotional stamina.

"It's my birthday," I blurt.

Sasha looks at me in surprise. "Really? Happy birthday."

"Not really," I say.

"It's not really your birthday or it's not really happy?"

"The second one."

For a split second she looks almost sympathetic. "Are

you bummed about getting kicked out of school? All the cool kids are doing it, you know."

"If you're talking about me and Jude Holz, I don't think *cool*'s the right adjective."

She raises a dark slash of an eyebrow. "Jude got expelled, too? Our darling little school mascot?"

"Yeah. It wasn't him wearing the tiger head, though, just like it wasn't me who posted the picture. But neither of us could prove it."

"Didn't Parker know who he was partying with? Couldn't he have said that wasn't Jude under the tiger head?"

"According to Jude, Parker's testimony was something along the lines of 'I was so drunk it could have been Tinkerbell under that head.' He had no idea who was with him that night." I kick halfheartedly at the cinder-block wall. "Principal Dekum's zero tolerance policy blows."

Sasha smiles. "I'm out, too. Does that make you feel better?"

"You *are*? What for?"

"It's a long and boring story. The important thing is that this is a momentous occasion. They've never had this many expulsion hearings at once. Think of it—you're part of Arlington High School history."

"Great. Scandal and infamy is what I've always been after."

Her blue eyes bore into mine. "What are you going to miss?"

"Uh, final exams?"

"No, I mean miss as in *long for*."

What I longed for had nothing to do with school. I shrug.

Sasha nods like the matter's settled. "There you go. You're better off. Summer vacation starts three weeks early for you. You can, like, lie around in your basement with Jude and play Dark Souls 3 or whatever."

"That's not what I want to—"

"I said *or whatever*." And then she pops her earbuds back in and opens her book, like I've just been dismissed. Which I guess I have.

As I walk away down the hall, though, I feel the tiniest bit better. If getting expelled could have a *sliver* of a silver lining, it'd be having something in common with Sasha Ellis.

3

I don't expect a homemade birthday cake with seventeen candles waiting for me on the kitchen counter when I get home, which is good, because there isn't one.

There's only a note.

> *Theo,*
>   *I had to go back to work. I'm sorry,*
> *but the freezer's a wonderland of dinner*
> *options. Just don't eat all the salted*
> *caramel ice cream or there'll be hell*
> *to pay.*
>   *Love you to pieces,*
>   *Mom*

I honestly don't think she knows what day it is, and I don't blame her—she's seriously overextended. She works at a bank all day, and at night she does bookkeeping for a bunch of local churches. Once I asked her if she felt hypocritical, seeing as how she'd been a socialist atheist at UCLA, and she told me that if I had any more stupid questions I could keep them to my wiseass self.

Maybe I thought she'd hold on to me tighter now it's just the two of us left. But mostly it seems like the opposite. Like she's running away from the memory of him and the reality of me—both. Sometimes I think I'll wake up one day and she'll be gone. Not dead, like Dad. Just *not here*.

It's probably not healthy, but I try not to think about him too much—otherwise, I don't know if I could even get out of bed in the mornings. No one told me that sadness hurt. Like all the way into your bones.

I take a lot more Advil than I used to. I sleep more, too. Unconsciousness, like ignorance, is bliss.

I'm heating up a frozen burrito when a text comes in from my friend Jude.

So?

Just typing the word expelled makes my appetite instantly vanish. I don't want to talk to him, either, so I turn off my phone, chuck my burrito into the trash, and head outside. It's dark now, and everyone's holed up in their

15

little ranch houses, blue TV light flickering against the closed curtains.

I walk east toward the edge of town, feeling twitchy and depressed. For a long time it seemed like nothing had ever happened to me—that my life was a boring but fundamentally acceptable slog toward graduation and my supposed bright future, whatever that was.

But in the last few months it seems like a lot of things have happened, and none of them have been good. Some, on the other hand, have been downright horrific.

So what the hell am I supposed to do now? If I can't take my exams, I'll fail my junior year. And then what? Will I be stuck here forever? Probably the answer to that question is yes. Because what college wants a kid who flunked grade eleven? Certainly I won't be scholarship material anymore—and without a scholarship, college is a financial impossibility.

My mood grows even darker. Maybe I should just give up and start working at the 7-Eleven with all the other juvies. Maybe it'd be less painful to crush my own dreams before the world does it for me.

My aimless, agitated wandering eventually brings me to the city park I used to play in. Someone's shot out the streetlights again, so the sad little swing set and the plastic tube slide that's knocked out the front teeth of generations of six-year-olds are just dim, lonely shadows.

At the far end of the park is the Pinewood water tower, surrounded by chain-link fencing and NO TRESPASSING signs. Jude says there's a hole in the fence, hidden by blackberry bushes, and that if you can stand a few scratches you can get in.

And sure enough, he's right. I make it through the chain link with only a little thorn-induced blood loss, and then I'm standing at the base of the water tower. The ladder stops about five feet above the ground, but I can grab the bottom rung and swing my legs up.

Now comes the hard part—the part I never thought I'd have the guts to try.

Gritting my teeth, I haul myself up the ladder, counting the rungs to keep from flipping out over how high I'm getting. Three-quarters of the way to the top, the wind picks up, and the porch lights seem to spin below me. I take a deep breath and keep going, *156, 157, 158.*

Suddenly I can't go any farther.

Not up, not down. My arms and legs quiver and throb.

I close my eyes tight. Will myself to keep breathing. *It's only a few more feet, Theo,* I tell myself, which is a lie because it's ten yards at least.

But somehow I manage to start to climb again. And in another few moments, I'm on the deck of the water tower, breathless and awed. I'm all alone on top of the world—that's what it feels like.

There's a metal walkway all around the water tank itself and a railing to keep me from falling to my death. I sit down, my back against the tank. My feet dangle over the edge, and my heels touch thin air.

Behind me are spray-painted messages from those who climbed before me: *Fuck school, Jason loves Lindsay, Billy is a Boner Sniffer*. Down below, everything is different shades of darkness: the bluish black of the streets, the charcoal black of the trees, the glittering black of car hoods. Above me, it's nothing but stars.

When I was ten, a senior from Arlington took a swan dive off this tower. I shudder at the memory, but I can't help wondering how he did it. How he coaxed himself to the edge and then leapt into the air.

How, in this case, is an easier question than why.

But that's what I'd ask my dad if I could: *Why'd you do it?*

I know the how, after all, because I was the one who found him—and the gun.

4

I stay up there on the water tower for a long time. At first I'm tripping on the silence and beauty—the swooping bats, the faraway stars—but pretty soon I'm just working up the courage to leave.

Don't look down, don't look down—I told myself that while climbing up. The problem with descent, though, is that you *have* to look down.

By the time I make it back to earth in one piece, my head's spinning, my legs are shaking, and I've lost all feeling in my fingers. I reek of fear sweat. I rip my shirt in the blackberry bushes.

In other words, it's time to call it a night.

So I really can't explain why I don't go home. Why I start

walking in the opposite direction instead, past the Shell station at the corner of Pine and Osage, which is the dividing line between the nice side of town and the less nice side. The Shell's also where you can shoulder-tap for beer if your fake ID sucks. Mine—a gift from Jude—looks like a first grader made it with Scotch tape and crayons, and it should go without saying that I've never been dumb enough to try to use it.

On the nice side of town, big elm trees line the streets and the houses are Tudors instead of ranches. Automated sprinklers mist the lawns and gardens, and I swear the air feels cleaner. Cooler.

This is Sasha's side of town.

A left, then a right, and this is Sasha's street.

And now I've obviously gone crazy, because I'm walking up the pathway to her front door.

And knocking on it.

On a list of things I thought I'd one day do, this would be pretty near the absolute bottom—like, *become Batman* might be the only thing below it.

The door swings open, and there's a tall, dark-haired man looking at me coldly. "Good evening," he says. "Can I help you?"

"Oh! Uh," I say, taking a big step backward in surprise. *What were you expecting, Theo—Sasha in a skimpy nightgown, asking you to tuck her in?*

"You don't look like the Domino's guy, so I'm going to guess you're here to see Sasha," the man says. "Would you like to come in?" The way he asks it makes it seem like he wants me to say no.

"Uh," I say, because I'm a miracle of eloquence. "Please?"

He sighs and reluctantly opens the door a few inches wider. "Sasha's in the kitchen."

And just like that, I'm in Sasha Ellis's house. And there she is, almost within arm's reach: she's sitting on a bench in a little breakfast nook, and she's knitting.

Knitting.

I don't know why, but this strikes me as highly bizarre. I thought knitting was for little old ladies and people who need to fake productivity when they're binge-watching *Game of Thrones,* not for brilliant seventeen-year-olds who barely ever take their noses out of works of great literature.

The other weird thing is that Sasha looks different. Smaller somehow, and maybe even younger. She's wearing sweats and a pair of fluffy white slippers. When she glances up at me, her expression is wary. "Hi," she says. She slides her needles and yarn into a basket under the table and crosses her arms across her chest.

"We were just talking about the poetry of Theodore Roethke." Sasha's dad pours expensive-looking whiskey into a heavy crystal tumbler. "Cheers," he says. He lifts the glass at me and takes a sip.

"*He* was talking about the poetry of Theodore Roethke," Sasha corrects.

" 'The whiskey on your breath / Could make a small boy dizzy; / But I hung on like death: / Such waltzing was not easy,' " he quotes. Then he turns to me, smiling icily, and suddenly he doesn't look like a small-town dad; he looks like a really handsome actor *impersonating* a small-town dad. It's unsettling. He's also possibly drunk.

"Matthew's a lit professor," Sasha explains. "It's important not to encourage him, because otherwise he'll go on quoting poetry all night."

Matthew—or maybe I should call him Professor Ellis, since his own daughter calls him by his first name—swirls the ice in his glass. "Well, it's not as if you need to wake up early for school, my pet."

"Touché," Sasha says. "Theo got expelled, too, you know."

"Yes, but I—" I start.

"I've got two delinquents in my kitchen?" Matthew exclaims. "My cup runneth over. Sasha thinks she's too smart for school. Tell me, young man, are you of the same opinion?"

I wasn't, but I didn't want to have a conversation about it. I was sorry I'd come.

"I should probably go," I say. "It's late."

Matthew shrugs, then turns to top off his glass. "Whatever floats your dinghy," he says, his voice the epitome of apathy.

I meet Sasha's eyes. "Youshouldcomehangoutwithus tomorrow." I say this in a rush, before I lose courage.

"What?"

"Me and Jude—"

"Jude and I," Matthew interrupts.

I swear I can practically hear Jude's voice: *Dude, that's a grammar cockblock!*

I grab a pen and Post-it from the counter and scribble down an address. "Here," I say. "If you want to. If you can. If you..." I let the sentence die.

Sasha takes the note and folds it into a tiny square. "Thanks," she says.

"Sure," I say. "See you soon."

Even though I doubt I will.

It'd be a miracle if Sasha Ellis showed up tomorrow, and everybody knows there's no such thing.

5

I have to unlock three deadbolts and jiggle a funky door-knob in exactly the right way to get into Jude's house. Then I return the spare keys to their various garden hiding places before tiptoeing down the hall and up the stairs. (Why Jude's lock-obsessed parents plant spare keys *all over their yard* remains one of life's minor mysteries.)

Jude's still asleep, with a pillow over his face.

"Rise and shine, Tiger," I say, kicking the foot of his bed.

Jude sits up, looks over at the clock, and then picks it up like he's going to throw it at me. "You have *got* to be kidding," he says. "We don't have to go to school, but you roll up here at six fucking thirty? What is *wrong* with you?"

"I couldn't sleep," I say.

"What does that have to do with me?"

"I bought you coffee," I say. This is a lie: I bought *myself* coffee. But I set it on his bedside table because waking him up was a dick move—I can admit that.

Jude gives a big theatrical sigh and throws off his covers to reveal a pair of blue-and-white striped pajamas.

"Nice jammies, dude."

He gives me the finger. "This is a two-hundred-dollar Paul Smith sleeping ensemble, FYI, and it's nicer than the tux you would've worn to the prom had you (a) not gotten expelled and (b) managed to find a girl dumb enough to go with you."

"What are you doing with shit that expensive?" I ask. "Forget my nonexistent tux—those pj's are worth more than your car."

"I have a rich uncle," Jude says. "He knows I like the finer things in life, even if I can't afford them."

"Rich uncle sounds suspicious," I say.

Jude rolls his eyes. "Don't be gross. He's my mom's half brother, and I haven't seen him since I was eight. Now close your eyes while I change so you aren't blinded by all *this*," he says while gesturing up and down.

I roll my eyes and turn to stare at Jude's wall, which he's covered with a huge hallucinatory mural that took him two whole years to paint. I've never taken acid, but if I look long enough at Jude's mural, I start to feel like I have. There are people with frog heads, birds with lizard scales, and flowers with tiny leering faces hidden in their petals. It somehow manages to be both beautiful and scary as hell, and I hope Jude's done changing soon because it's starting to freak me out.

Jude's dog, Alfie, appears in the doorway. Alfie's small, white, and so hideously cute that Jude won't walk him anymore because he can't go three feet without someone asking to take his picture.

The secret to Alfie is that he's a total pervert. He gives my leg a cursory sniff and then goes into the corner, where he carefully straddles one of Jude's old stuffed animals, a faded pink pig with a ratty blue bow around its neck. I know exactly what's going to happen next, and sure enough...

"Alfie's humping Sex Pig again," I say.

"He's always horny in the morning," Jude says. "Also, he and Sex Pig are in love. Okay, you can turn around now."

Jude is dressed in cut-off jean shorts, vintage tube socks, and a T-shirt that says CEREAL KILLER, which is so fluorescent yellow it's like being punched in the eye.

"I just can't believe it," I say.

"Believe what?" Jude asks. "How cool this T-shirt is?"

"That we aren't going to school."

"I know! We can drive to El Molino Central and eat, like, twelve breakfast tacos, and then we can—"

"But we're not guilty!" I yell. I feel suddenly nauseated, and whether it's from lack of sleep or the prospect of my new dead-end life I can't tell.

"No one ever said life was fair," Jude says. "Look at us. I'm the one with the social charms and the excellent fashion sense, but somehow *you* have the looks. That's not fair to me, is it?"

"I honestly don't even know what you're talking about." I whisper this because now we're creeping past his parents' bedroom.

"Also, I have a car," Jude says, "and you have only your legs and, like, a shitty ten-speed."

"Zelda is a 1987 Chevette that tops out at forty-five miles an hour," I point out. "It's barely a car."

"Zelda is a she, not an it," Jude says. "And if you're going to insult her, she won't take you to tacos." He grabs his keys from the kitchen counter. "Why should I spend my time solving quadratic equations or memorizing the preamble to the Constitution? That's what the internet's for. And you—you're way too good for high school. Getting kicked out was the best thing that ever happened to us."

He sounds so convinced that for one millisecond I almost believe him.

"This is going to be the summer of our lives," he says. "Trust me."

I want to. But I know Jude well enough to tell when he's bullshitting. And I'm pretty sure that deep down inside he's just as scared as I am.

6

A few miles outside of town, Jude makes a left, and Zelda bumps down a narrow gravel road, making me regret that last taco. The switchgrass and the wild sweet peas have gone crazy since I was last here, and they're overgrown enough to brush against the car doors.

We drive another potholed half mile, and then we're on the Property: the land my parents bought right after they got married. When I was a kid, I thought it was the most beautiful place in the world.

There's a five-acre pond ringed by oaks and willows and cattails, a screened-in gazebo filled with ratty old furniture and a mini fridge, and a big weathered wooden deck that looks over the blue-green water.

My parents always talked about building their dream house out here someday. My mom wanted chickens, a garden, and a sunporch bathed in light. My dad joked that all he cared about was being able to walk out his front door and piss in the yard without any neighbors harassing him. But his plans were much bigger than that: at night he'd draw up sketches, each one more amazing than the last. *Your room will be over the library, Theo,* he'd say. *You'll have your own private second-story porch, right here on the other side of these French doors…*

He was a dreamer, and I loved to believe his wild, wonderful ideas: a game room, a secret passageway between the living room and the library, a special cozy sunroom for my mom to call her own.

I don't know what's going to happen with the Property now that he's gone. The dream house is out—that much is obvious. But what about the land itself, those acres of trees and meadow? What about the pond, where we used to fish?

I'm afraid these might be just more things I have to lose.

Jude opens a couple of lawn chairs out on the deck. It's just after 8 a.m., and the air's still cool and full of birdsong. Every once in a while a fish breaks the still surface of the water.

"Here's the plan," Jude says, settling into a sagging canvas lounge chair. "I'm going to paint all summer long. I'm going to paint so much and so well that I'll be rich and famous by the time I'm eighteen, so it won't matter at all that I was basically forced to drop out of high school." He crosses his arms like this is a foolproof strategy as opposed to pie-in-the-sky fantasy. "What's your goal?"

"I want to go back in time and make all of this not happen," I say.

"I hate to break it to you, but that's impossible," Jude says.

"Not much less impossible than your idea," I counter.

"Screw you for your lack of faith."

"Screw you for being so optimistic about everything."

Jude sighs. "Theo, the glass is *half full*."

"Oh, sure," I say. "It's half full of shit."

Jude throws up his hands. "Lighten up, Theo! It's a beautiful day, and our stomachs are full of amazing tacos. Can't you just enjoy this for a second?"

"Stop acting like everything's going to be okay!" I shout. "What about college? Do you think Cornell University accepts kids who get kicked out of school? Do you—"

"Is that where you want to go?" Jude interrupts.

"I don't know! I don't know anything! Except that I know that I need a *scholarship*, and getting expelled has ruined my chances of getting one. And what about you?

You think RISD's going to be like 'Oh, this Jude kid's a decent painter, but what we're *really* stoked about is his convict past'?"

"RISD's school mascot is a giant penis named Scrotie," he says.

I feel like pounding my head against the deck. "What does that have to do with anything?"

"I'm just saying I wouldn't want to be *that* mascot."

"I don't think you should act like everything's fine," I say. "Because it's not. We are completely and totally screwed."

Jude sighs. "I know, okay? But I'm trying to keep our spirits up. That's a mascot's job, remember? Go team!" He raises a halfhearted fist in the air. "Although we're not even big enough for a team. We're just a *duo*."

"Well, I invited Sasha to come here, too," I say. "So if hell freezes over, there might be three of us."

I hear Jude's sharp inhale. "Way to nard up, Theo Foster! What'd she say?"

"I don't know. Nothing."

"She didn't text you back?"

"I didn't text. I asked her in person."

"In *person?*" Jude's incredulous. "Who *does* that anymore?"

I put my head in my hands. I don't know what to say. I still feel sick, and I don't know how to make anything better. "Dude, what are we supposed to do now?" I mean this in an existential way—like how are we going to deal with our ruined lives—but Jude takes it literally.

"Let's watch YouTube supercuts," he says. "I saw one that's all about improbable movie weapons, and it was amazing because Clive Owen murders a guy by stabbing him in the face with a carrot."

"Uh…"

"And Vin Diesel kills a dude with a teacup. Hello? What, does that not appeal to you?"

But it's not that.

Sasha's car is pulling up.

7

"*No effing way,*" *Jude says.* "*Hell* hath frozen over."

The weird, unpleasant churning in my stomach I've felt ever since yesterday gets exponentially worse. I can't believe she came, and I'm really glad she did. But I wish she didn't have to see me like this: sleep deprived and full of nard-shrinking dread about my future.

I jump up, waving, grinning despite myself. "Hey! Sasha! Over here!"

This is idiotic—obviously she can see us. A person could see Jude's shirt from outer space.

Sasha waves back with a lot more decorum. She's wearing a dark blue dress and oversized sunglasses that cover most of her face. *I invited Sasha Ellis to the Property—*

and she actually came. There is, without a doubt, a thin but bright silver lining to being kicked out of school.

But then *Parker Harris* gets out of Sasha's car, so I have to take that feeling back.

Parker reaches into the backseat and pulls out a large white box with a gold star on it. He looks about as thrilled to see us as I am to see him.

"Terrible," Jude whispers to me, eyes on Parker. "Nothing ruins an otherwise perfect physical specimen like a pair of cargo shorts."

Sasha steps onto the deck. "My dad's sleeping one off, so I took twenty bucks from his wallet. We brought Gold Star doughnuts."

"Oh, my God, Gold Star's the best," Jude says. "Have you tried the Kevin Bacon? It's a jelly doughnut wrapped in bacon, and it sounds gross but it's totally the opposite."

"He won't miss it?" I ask. My mom watches every nickel—not because she thinks I'd steal anything but because she's got to save everything she can.

"Please. He has no idea," Sasha says. "But he'd give me five times that if I asked. He'd tell me to buy myself something pretty."

"Must be nice," I mumble.

Parker sets the box on the deck. Then he reaches down and adjusts himself, like his junk's so big and untamed it won't stay in the right place. "All this yours?" he asks me, nodding at the pond and the trees. "It's like a state park."

"It's only a few acres," I say. It's actually more like twenty-five, but for some reason I feel like downplaying it. Like I don't want him to know anything about it.

"It's gorgeous," Sasha says, lifting a cruller from the box. "I love it here."

Although these might be six of the most wonderful words I've ever heard, it doesn't make up for the fact that she brought Parker.

"Here's to summer starting three weeks early," Jude says. He knocks his doughnut against Sasha's, as if they're wineglasses. "*Prost!* That means 'Cheers.'" He's still on the team-spirit train, I guess.

Sasha lifts her sunglasses and looks at him like he's weird, which he is. But it's not a mean look—it's more like *puzzled*.

Parker doesn't grab a doughnut. Instead he takes a slug from a Mason jar full of brownish sludge. It's probably a protein shake made with flaxseeds, raw eggs, and wolf's blood. Then he wipes his mouth with the back of his paw and peers into the gazebo. "Couch, table, mini fridge… All you need's a sixty-four-inch flat screen and a Lakers game and this place wouldn't suck, amirite?"

I don't answer. I have decided to pretend like Parker doesn't exist.

I watch as Sasha breaks her cruller into small pieces and picks at the crumbs. Her skin is very pale, and there are faint bluish shadows under her eyes. She looks sort of romantically macabre, if there can be such a thing.

No one says anything. We just listen to one another chewing.

After a while, Sasha breaks the silence. "This is mildly awkward," she says.

"No kidding," Jude says. "It's like—have you guys seen *The Breakfast Club*?"

Sasha shakes her head.

"Yeah, I'm into movies my *mom* watched in high school," Parker says, his voice thick with sarcasm and testosterone.

If I were fifty pounds heavier, I'd be big enough to sucker-punch him and run. Seventy-five and I could stick around to get my ass kicked.

But Jude doesn't pay attention to Parker. "It's about these five kids who are in detention together, but they have nothing in common," he says. "Sort of like us, right? Just because we've all been expelled doesn't make us best friends."

"No shit, Tigger," Parker says and tosses back another eight ounces of jock shake in one gulp.

Of course in the movie the kids *do* all become friends. They discover the meaning of life and the meaninglessness of stereotypes or whatever. But there's no point in mentioning that—it's not going to work that way for us.

"You at least got a PS3 out here?" Parker asks.

"Sorry, bro," I say. There's a heavy dose of irony in my use of the word *bro,* but I don't think Parker hears it. I truly can't understand why Sasha ever dated him, and I don't get how she can tolerate him now.

Sasha turns to me, blue eyes flashing. "I took all the money from the Coke machines," she says.

I say, "What?"

"You asked me what I did to get expelled. That's what they said I did."

"How'd you do it?" Jude asks. "Hit 'em with a crowbar? Let me see them arms, girl."

Sasha dodges so Jude can't check her biceps. "I was student treasurer, so I had the keys. I was supposed to clean out the change and restock the sodas, which I did. I left the money in a locked box in the student council office, and the next morning it was gone."

"Did you see anything suspicious the night before?" Jude asks.

"Are we on *True Detective* or something?" I say.

Jude grins. "I always thought I had a certain Colin Farrell je ne sais quoi."

"I don't know what happened," Sasha says, suddenly sounding angry. "All I know is that I don't need to steal eighty pounds of quarters!"

"Yeah, since your dad's wallet is a never-ending supply of twenties," Jude says, sounding wistful.

"I have a *job*," Sasha snaps. "My dad has nothing to do with it."

"Wow, okay," Jude says. He puts a placating hand on her knee, but she shakes him off. "So the takeaway here," he says slowly, "is that Parker's the only guilty one."

"And somehow the only one still in school," Parker says.

"What do you mean?" I ask.

Parker picks up a doughnut, sniffs it longingly, and then puts it back down again. "I'm going to Chase Academy."

"You're kidding," Jude says. "How the hell did you pull that off? Can you actually *read*?"

"It's called writing a fat check," Parker says. "Probably your parents can't do that."

"They can," Jude says. "It'd just bounce."

I clench my hands into fists. I can't believe it: the only person who's actually guilty is the only one who *isn't* getting punished.

"Private school's fancy," Jude muses. "I wonder if they make cravats for necks as thick as yours."

"Proud to say I don't know what a fucking cravat is," Parker says.

The day's just getting worse and worse. I throw the rest of my doughnut into the weeds; let the goddamn squirrels have it.

Then Sasha stands up and brushes the crumbs off her dress. "Well, you guys, it's been real, but I have to get to work. Parker, you coming?"

Parker's on his feet in a hot second. "Later, bitches," he says.

Bitterly I watch them go. Right before she gets into the car, Sasha turns around and winks at me—a gesture I find as confusing as her tolerance of Parker Harris.

"I really don't get it," I say as they pull away.

"Sasha Ellis has always been a mystery to you," Jude says. "Why would today be any different?"

"I don't know. Shit changes," I say.

"And the more shit changes, the more it remains the same."

Maybe. But I have to say, the way my life's been going, it seems to me that shit *doesn't* remain the same.

It just gets generally worse.

8

Early Monday morning, when I should've been on my way to the soul-sucking boredom of homeroom, I go to Five Points Coffee instead. It's right across the street from Arlington, which means I can torture myself by watching the approximately 1,196 kids who *didn't* get expelled make their way into school.

I mean, just because school sucks doesn't mean I don't want to go.

As I scan the crowd filing in through the big double doors, I wonder: Did one of those people post the picture? If so, what was their motive? Did someone want to get me in trouble, even more than Parker? Do I, as Palmieri asked, have an *enemy*?

If I do, then my high school social strategy has been a bust. I spent three years trying to be Switzerland: neutral, and maybe just a little bit above it all. I wanted to be somewhere between inoffensive and downright *nice* to almost every single person in that institution.

But obviously I went wrong at some point. I have the expulsion to prove it.

Larry the barista eyes me darkly from behind the counter, and I throw him a half wave as I put a dollar in the can for the self-serve house coffee. Larry's not one for niceness; when Mike, the owner, comes in, he'll give free coffee to anyone who can make Larry smile. As far as I know, only Jude and I have ever been able to do it. We save up stupid jokes to tell him when we're broke.

Despite Larry taking the term *coffee jerk* literally, Five Points is a nice place, with fast Wi-Fi and twenty-five-cent refills; you can caffeinate yourself to a dangerous degree for under three bucks. It was the place I came after school to tweet from @ArlingtonConfessions.

I always thought the secret account was fun, like a goofy public service: a place for kids to vent about school or spread (mostly) harmless gossip.

But it seems so stupid now.

> Rumor has it TCT went home drunk enough last weekend to introduce self to own dad #oops #grounded

That was the last tweet I sent. The next post was the Picture, and after that the proverbial shit hit the proverbial fan with truly stunning force.

Larry, who's bussing a table next to me, tosses the *Pinewood Register* into my lap. It's open to the Opinion page—which has my face emblazoned on it. My stomach gives a lurch as I pick up the paper.

Good Kids Gone Bad? the headline asks. Below it are blowups of our junior class photos: me, Jude, and Parker. Because none of us is really smiling, it looks like a row of mug shots.

They say a picture is worth a thousand words, the columnist writes. *But one racy picture was worth three expulsions. Was one night's fun worth compromising entire futures?*

I close up the paper. I can confidently say that the answer to that question is no.

Then Jenna Tucker and Lulu Trinh saunter into Five Points, mid-giggle. Until four days ago we were in government class together.

Jenna and Lulu are nice girls—second tier, socially speaking, like me and Jude—and now they're standing by the pastry case, debating what baked good to split.

"Live it up, you guys," I say glumly. "Get your own bear claw."

Jenna turns around, sees me, and immediately looks surprised. "Hey, Theo," she says after a tiny pause.

Lulu elbows her. She's trying to look anywhere but at me.

"I'm sorry about...you know," Jenna says, and then Lulu grabs her arm and spins her around so their backs are to me again.

"Expulsion isn't contagious, Lulu," I call. But she pretends like she doesn't hear me.

This little interaction has made it perfectly clear: I'm no longer on the second tier. The only question now is how far down I've fallen.

I watch out the window as the two of them hurry to class, and a moment later I see Palmieri pulling up in his late model Mustang. It's a pretty serious muscle car for an assistant principal, but—as everyone who's ever spoken to him for more than thirty seconds knows—he was a champion wrestler in high school, and maybe the car helps him relive the glory days.

He climbs out of the Mustang with a take-out coffee and a grin. I don't know why he looks so pumped, considering his school's been in the news for ten days straight.

Some Arlington kids make fun of Palmieri for his shiny dress shirts and his irritating CrossFit habit of high-fiving people as they stand in line for the salad bar. I never had a problem with Palmieri, though—not until now. He could have been on my side during that hearing, when I was alone and defenseless. But instead he stood with the school board robots, and because of that, I'd really like to slash the tires of his ridiculous car.

I'm not going to do that, obviously, because I'm in enough trouble already. I'm just going to get some more coffee.

I dig a quarter out of my pants and go to put it into the refill cup. But suddenly Larry's blocking my way, as big and imposing as a bear in flannel.

"Hey, Larry," I say. "Did you hear the one about the guy who takes his pet octopus to—"

"No," Larry says.

"Okay, well, they go to this bar, and the guy says—"

"No," Larry says again.

He's taking unfriendly to the next level here, but I can roll with it. I've got other jokes—*and* coffee money.

"So the funny thing about pandas is—"

Larry says, "Enough, kid."

"What's the matter?" I ask, confused now.

Larry's lip curls in disgust. "Think about that girl. It's terrible what you did with her picture."

I sink down into the nearest chair. "Larry, I didn't post—"

But Larry won't let me finish a single sentence. "You've

had enough coffee, kid," he says. "So go on home now. And don't bother coming back."

I don't have it in me to protest anymore. I'm banned from my high school and banned from Pinewood's only decent coffee shop. Obviously I'm not even *on* the social ladder anymore. I've fallen into the bottomless pit beneath it.

9

"*I think we have an enemy,*" I say to Jude's back.

We're in his garage, and I'm watching him work on a giant canvas jumbled with figures and text and dripping paint. It reminds me a little of Jean-Michel Basquiat's paintings.

Jude scribbles black paint across the surface, obscuring the face of a creature that may or may not be Alfie, the stuffed-animal humper. He doesn't turn around. "I think you're crazy," he says.

"But how else do you explain what happened?" I demand. "I mean, somebody *stole* your tiger head from the locker room. And then whoever that was got so wasted he whipped his dick out in front of an iPhone. And *that* someone uploaded the picture to—"

"Yeah, I understand the chain of events," Jude interrupts.

"Let me finish. Someone put a *fake you* on *my* secret Twitter—which was obviously not very secret. And then, simple as that, we both got expelled. No questions asked. So whoever posted that snapshot nailed two people for the price of one."

"Three if you count Parker," Jude reminds me.

I ignore this because I don't count him. "The point is, how could that be an accident?" I ask Jude's back.

"Maybe whoever put on the tiger head wasn't trying to impersonate me for nefarious reasons. Maybe he just did it for kicks. I mean, wearing a tiger head is more fun than you might think. You should try it sometime."

What *I* think is that Jude's being naive. "Why would you assume the theft of your tiger head was harmless?" I ask. "It wasn't a victimless crime!"

Jude spins around. "Because it's crucial to my sanity, Theo. I don't need to be more paranoid about things than I already am. Look at me—I'm a sixteen-year-old bisexual virgin in a Hello Kitty T-shirt. Do you think it's a piece of cake to be me?"

I pick up two of his brushes and bang them against the wall of the garage like drumsticks. "No, and I didn't say it was. It's not easy to be the guy with the dead dad, either, you know. And I kind of think it's harder now that I've been kicked out. Don't you?"

Jude shakes his head. "I don't miss being called fag in the hallways, which is something that still happened almost daily, despite Arlington's Gay-Straight Alliance club and the rainbow flag over the counselor's office. What's that hanging there for anyway? Is it some kind of signal—like, hey, if you're questioning your sexuality, you should probably get some therapy?"

Jude has a point. I know high school hasn't been simple for him. But again—it's not like my life's been a walk in the park lately, either. After my dad died, there were three whole weeks I barely got out of bed. I didn't eat, and I hardly slept. I just lay there, silent and unweeping, like I was nearly dead myself.

Come to think of it, it's a miracle I didn't get expelled for lack of attendance back then.

And when I did finally get up? For months I felt like a zombie—a numb, moaning, half alive thing with only a vague memory of having once been a real person.

I still have to fight that feeling sometimes.

"But you'll fail junior year," I remind him. "Then won't you have to spend a whole extra year dealing with that homophobic BS?"

"I won't," he says firmly. "Remember the plan: I'm

going to paint my way to success and happiness. I'll get a GED if I have to. Have you read about the kid they call the mini Monet? He's worth, like, four million, and he's only twelve."

"Well, *I* don't have your talent," I say. "Or your absurd level of faith. So I'm a little more concerned."

He turns back to his work. "If you believe it, you can achieve it," he insists. But then his voice shifts, and it sounds almost sad. "I can be realistic about some things. Here's one: you can't take on the school board and win, Theo. You want to go back there and tell them what a nice person you really are? Say you have no idea who posted the picture but you were totally framed? That you have some secret nemesis? Do you really think Palmieri would buy it? Hey, maybe you'd like to write a persuasive essay. You were always good at that."

"How come that doesn't sound like a compliment?"

"Sorry." Jude sighs. "We aren't Boy Scouts or amateur sleuths, Theo. We aren't men of action. We never have been. We're men of acceptance and contemplation."

"Speak for yourself," I say, turning and walking down the driveway. "I'm going to find out who did this to us."

10

East of town, near the tiny municipal airport, is the shopping complex that's sucking the lifeblood out of downtown Pinewood with chain stores dedicated to sheets, discount shoes, and the kind of clothing Jude tells me is called athleisure. It's an awful place: treeless, bordered by a slow, silty river, and everywhere you look someone's waving a sign that says DISCOUNT MATTRESSES or LITTLE CAESAR'S HOT-N-READY $5.

The one good thing about this corporate wasteland is that Sasha Ellis works here, at Matheson's, which is like a low-rent version of Target.

I have one goal for today, which is to convince her that she has to join me in taking back our lives.

"Just don't act like a creepy stalker," says Jude. I managed to badger him into driving me over here despite his lack of enthusiasm.

"I won't. I just want to talk to her," I say.

"*Again* with the weird face-to-face thing," he says.

"I don't actually have her number," I admit, and Jude shakes his head like I'm too dumb to be believed.

The store is cold and bright, and it's like I've got some kind of homing beacon thing going on because I see Sasha instantly: checkout lane 10, between the Starbucks outpost and the customer service desk.

"We should probably buy something," I say.

"I don't have any money today," Jude says, as if he ever does.

We go to the discount section, where everything's a dollar or two. I pick out a sparkly pink notebook and a pair of the ugliest socks I've ever seen, which comes to three dollars for an excuse to talk to Sasha again.

I'd pay much more than that if I had to.

"Why are you getting that first-grade notebook and those tie-dyed burnout socks?" Jude wonders.

"Because they're stupid and random, and they'll make her laugh." Pause. "I think."

Jude looks mildly impressed. "Do I detect a hint of insight into pickup technique? How could this be? You've never been able to flirt with *any* girl, let alone the girl for whom the term 'resting bitch face' was coined."

"First of all, that's not nice, and second of all, I'm the one who said 'Shit changes.' "

"And yet you *continue* to maintain that getting expelled doesn't have an upside," Jude says, shaking his head.

When we go stand in Sasha's line, I can feel my pulse speeding up. Another checker waves us over to her empty lane, but we pretend not to see her.

I watch Sasha make small talk with the people in front of us, the way I used to watch her during lunch at school. She always sat in the back corner of the cafeteria, a stack of books next to her tray. When she was alone, her face would soften and take on a distant, almost wistful expression—like she went somewhere so far away from our insufferable high school that it wasn't even on the same map.

If anyone approached her, she'd stiffen almost imperceptibly. She *might* smile and talk to them, or she might not. Not was more likely. But either way, the message was clear (to me at least): *It'd be better for the both of us if you'd turn around and go back to your horsemeat sloppy joe, because I am reading* One Hundred Years of Solitude, *a masterwork whose towering literary achievement is beyond your puny adolescent comprehension.*

The difference today is that Sasha's on the clock, and being nice is part of the job. And while I can't say she looks thrilled, she's not beaming icy death rays at anyone, either.

I place my stupid pink notebook and my idiotic socks on the conveyor belt. As they slowly roll toward her, I feel like my heart's right there on the belt with them. It's already been shattered, it's basically taped back together, and it's worth, what, ten bucks? Twenty?

Whatever. She wouldn't want it even if it were free.

And I can understand that, because sometimes I'd rather not have it, either.

Also: *why* did I pick out those socks?

I'm such an asshat.

Sasha grabs the items and quickly, automatically scans them, and then she looks up and notices us.

"Oh, hey," she says. Her eyes seem to go suddenly cloudy. She touches her red apron, then drops her hand. She lifts her chin and straightens her shoulders. "Did you find everything you need today?" she asks. Her face is blank. She's definitely not laughing.

I hadn't thought past the selection of these dumb things. *Now* what's the joke? What am I supposed to say? *I bought the ugliest socks I've ever seen because I love you and I was hoping you'd think they were funny.* I don't think so.

"Yes, we *did* find everything, thank you!" Jude exclaims.

"Don't you just adore that notebook I picked out?" He flutters his lashes, hamming it up. "You know, I just can*not* deny myself a sparkly accessory."

Thank you, Jude, I think. Because now Sasha looks almost amused.

She says, "You should check out the sale on sun hats. There's a gold one that's nothing but sequins."

"Thanks for the tip, babe," he says and vanishes.

I know Jude wouldn't be caught dead in a sparkly accessory or a sun hat of any kind, but he wants to give me a minute alone with Sasha, and I'm grateful.

"That'll be three dollars," she says to me.

I hand over three crumpled bills. "It's kind of funny that Matheson's has a convicted thief operating the cash register," I say.

"Not *convicted*," she corrects. "Accused and expelled. But, yeah, the irony is reasonably thick."

"Does your boss know?"

"No, and she can't find out, because I'm not working the dressing room ever again. People *crap* in there, Theo."

"Seriously?"

She nods. "Poop's been found in basically every corner of this store."

Unconsciously I look down. The floor by my feet is polished and clean.

"I think you're safe," she says drily.

I can feel my cheeks getting hot. "For *now,*" I say, trying to make a joke of it. "But any second someone could run up here and drop a load on my shoes."

A woman behind me in line clears her throat. She's got a cart full of decorative throw pillows and Diet Coke two-liters that she's obviously impatient to purchase.

"But what if your boss *does* find out?" I ask. "What if you get demoted for something you didn't do? This whole situation is crazy and unfair. Don't you want to fight it?"

"It seems a little late for that," Sasha says.

"Yeah, I know it does. But when Palmieri accused me of posting the picture, I kept telling myself that I was innocent, which meant that everything would turn out okay. Didn't you think that, too? Didn't you trust that people would find out the truth? But then they didn't. They didn't even try."

"I'll be right with you, ma'am," Sasha calls to the woman behind me. "Goddamn pillow freak," she mutters, and then she turns her cool gaze back to me. "For your information, Theo, most people don't care about the truth as much as you do. And there are a lot of things people just don't want to know."

"What's that supposed to mean?"

She shrugs, dismissing the question. "So what do you suggest we do?" she asks.

"We launch an investigation."

"Listen, Sherlock, we had our hearings—"

"And we were *expelled,* though there was only *circumstantial evidence* against us!" I practically yell.

Sasha doesn't say anything for a minute. And then she says, "You do make a point."

"I have to be honest here," I say. "My life sucked plenty before all this, and I have the holes I punched in my closet to prove it. And now it's worse, and frankly that's not okay with me. I want life to return to its customary level of suckage, stat."

Sasha smiles then. It's not a very big one, but I think it's real. "Okay," she says. "Fine. Let's get your life back to its familiar suck status. Now get the hell out of here before you get me fired."

"Okay," I say, "but first I'm going to need your phone number."

Sasha blinks at me. I can't believe I just demanded it like that—who am I to ask *anything at all* of the thrilling, terrifying Sasha Ellis? But then she grabs my receipt and quickly scribbles down ten digits. I hold my breath as I take the paper from her small, cool hand.

"Thanks," I whisper—like she's given me something precious. Which in some small way she has.

"Whatever," she says, rolling her eyes. "Go."

11

Later I make Jude drop me off at the Property, because it's a nicer place to be alone than my empty house. Dinner is a box of graham crackers and a crumbling wedge of prehistoric cheddar that I discover in the back of the mini fridge. Honestly, it's no less depressing than the microwaved burritos I eat alone every other night.

I sit on the dock, watching the rippling water, until dusk turns everything a deep blue. Then I get up and go turn on all the lights in the gazebo.

There are literally hundreds: the rafters sag with strands of chili peppers, pineapples, cowboy boots, stars, fish, and cacti. My dad could never resist a box of novelty lights. He found them utterly hilarious—*and yet totally functional!* he'd add.

It's just another thing I'll never understand about him.

Not his love for something so stupid—I get that.

It's more like: how could someone so full of life, so ready to be thrilled, just…*go?*

I know the easy answer. A year ago he was diagnosed with ALS, which is pretty much the cruelest disease imaginable. Your motor neurons, which you need for muscle control, just start dying. First you can't hold a coffee cup. Then you can't stand up. Eventually you can't even breathe.

Also: there's no cure.

So my dad knew this wasn't a fight he could win.

But somehow the easy answer doesn't entirely cut it. That he would have died anyway, in two years or in ten, doesn't make things any less terrible. There was still the blood. The gun. The shattered back window of the car.

There was still me, age sixteen, finding him.

I don't have the words for that horror.

I don't think he meant it to happen that way. But once he was gone, he didn't have much say in the matter.

Sometimes I think my dad must have left me a note— just a few words to say that he was sorry, that he loved me, that he knew he was leaving the game of life early but he didn't like the look of the scoreboard.

I've searched for it, all over our house and all over the Property, and I've never found it. But who am I to say that it doesn't exist? People believe in all kinds of things they might never actually get to see.

I run my hand under the cushions of the couch, though I've done it a thousand times before. I find what I always find: crumbs, spare change, a fishing lure. And so what? It's not like a note would make me feel *better*.

It just might make me feel less numb.

But inside an old wooden trunk I find something I'd somehow missed before. It's a half empty bottle of Knob Creek whiskey—or, as Jude would describe it, half *full*.

I pick it up and give it a sniff. Alcohol doesn't go bad, does it? I'm probably supposed to sip it or something, the way Professor Ellis did, but I throw it back like a frat guy instead. It burns my throat, and warmth quickly spreads through my body.

I've had Jack and cokes at parties before, not that I went to that many. But I've never clutched a bottle of 100-proof whiskey by its neck, the way Parker did in that picture. Even now, when I can, I pour it into a chipped coffee mug. Do I have better manners than Parker, or am I just more of a wuss?

I know what *he'd* say.

Outside the crickets are making a racket, like they're having some kind of insect rager. But in here it's just me and the Knob Creek, so I might as well pour myself another glass. Mug. Whatever.

Bugs, attracted by the lights, fling themselves against the gazebo's screens. They're so loud they sound like raindrops.

Here's to you, Dad, I think, tossing a shot back. *I hope being dead has worked out for you. It's been pretty shitty for us, if you want to know the truth. Everything's a lot harder than it used to be.* I pour another shot—it's starting to go down easier. *I know it's dumb, but I can't help thinking there's been some big mistake, and that you're not really gone—you're just, like, out of the country or something. And then every single day I have to figure it out again: you're never coming back.*

I pace the gazebo, kicking up dust and fly carcasses. Someone really needs to sweep up around here.

It was my birthday the other day, Dad. Not that anyone celebrated. That's okay. I've decided to have my own party here tonight. It's a nontraditional birthday party—more of a pity party, really. But I don't mind. I'm out in the woods, hanging with a bunch of little arthropods, and I can hear some frogs, too, and there's probably at least one family of mice in the walls. And of course there's Mr. Knob Creek here. So I've got company. I'm not lonely. Not one bit.

Somehow talking to my dad is kind of nice. As if somewhere, in some other dimension, he might actually be able to hear it.

Like I said, we believe in plenty of things we might never see.

It's time for another whiskey—a big, generous pour this time. I'm pretty sure it's making me feel better.

I got expelled, in case you wondered. I don't even know if Mom remembers—that's how busy she is. But I think if you'd been here, then none of this would've happened. You would have defended me. You would have made them believe you. You would have been able to convince them that I was telling the truth.

I don't even notice the taste of the whiskey anymore.

Honestly, I'm pretty pissed about it all. I'm mad at a lot of people, including Palmieri and whoever did this to me. But I'm also mad at you. Let me say it again: if you'd been here, none of this would have happened. My life wouldn't even suck at all, because you would still be in it. Is that really too much to ask for—an okay life? Apparently it is.

I sit down on the couch and put the whiskey next to me like a friend. But first I take another slug. Then I close my eyes, just for a little bit...

12

There's a woodpecker hammering its beak into my temple.

I open my eyes. *Oh, God, that hurts.* The sun, burning through the gazebo screen and into my face, has just lit my eyeballs on fire.

My mouth tastes like something died in it.

Gritting my teeth, I manage to sit up. Blearily I reevaluate the situation and realize that the woodpecker is actually on the *roof,* not my head. The sun is still a blazing inferno, though. And every part of me aches.

What happened last night is clear: someone snuck into the gazebo, beat me with sticks, dragged me outside, and ran over me with a 4×4. Then whoever it was brought me back to the couch, took off my shoes, and threw a blanket over me.

I look around the gazebo, and right away I see the perpetrator of this violence: the whiskey bottle, lying in the corner. It's now incontrovertibly empty.

Dear God, I am never, *ever* going to do that again. Enough of the pity parties. The only way to make any of this better is to prove that I didn't post that picture.

I reach for my phone to call Jude. Every once in a while the satellites and weather patterns align and I can get a signal. But not today.

There's only one thing to do now. Only one way to get out of here.

It may not work, and it's also scary as shit.

Here goes nothing.

I hobble over to the old tin shed, which is where my mom keeps tools for the big garden she'll probably never have and where my dad kept his ancient dirt bike.

The bike is covered in a fine coat of dust and mouse droppings. I don't know if it runs anymore, and it's definitely not street legal. But it's currently my only option.

I roll the bike out of the shed and brush the dirt off the seat. The musty helmet squeezes my head like a vice.

Ignition, check. Choke on, carburetor throttle open. Clutch in.

I slam my foot down on the kick start, which sends

pain shooting through my entire body...and fails to start the engine.

It's probably just another symptom of my near-lethal hangover, but I feel like crying.

After three more kicks, though, the engine starts. And that's when the real agony begins. Between the rattling, shaking engine, the for-shit shock absorbers, and the rutted Property road—well, let's just say it's like riding a jackhammer. To hell.

Once I get to the highway, the bike runs a little smoother, and the wind in my face starts to wake me up. I race past fields and green hills, the sun glinting off the reflectors on the pavement. I can't say it's pleasant, but it *is* sort of cinematic.

Twenty minutes later I pull into Jude's driveway and cut the engine. He's in the garage, cleaning paintbrushes.

He squints at me. "On the one hand," he says thoughtfully, "it is legitimately badass to show up on a vintage dirt bike. On the other hand, that thing's like a dirtier, two-wheeled version of Zelda."

I pry the helmet from my head, and the ache inside my skull lessens infinitesimally.

"You look like shit," he observes.

"That is unsurprising," I say.

"You want some breakfast?"

I start to shake my head no, but it hurts too much. "I'd probably just throw it up again."

"Okay, what can I do for you, then? What do you want?"

"I want to prove that we're innocent."

Jude sighs. "*That* again."

"Yeah, that again. Remember how we were on the news every single night? They made us the poster children for teenage delinquency. How come no one ever held a mic up to us and said, 'What's your side of the story?'"

"Because they don't care. *Duh.*" Jude dips his paintbrush into a coffee can full of turpentine and swirls it around.

I grab his phone and turn it to video. "Today I'm talking to Jude Holz, a local painter and high school junior accused of *urinating* on school athletic equipment," I say in my best local anchorman impression. "Mr. Holz, what do you have to say for yourself?"

"Shut up?" Jude offers.

"Mr. Holz, on the night of May sixth, did you put on a tiger head and give Parker Harris's jersey a golden shower?"

He ignores me.

"Tell the truth, Mr. Holz. Did you drain your main vein on uniform number 89?"

Jude still doesn't say anything. He's trying to hold back a smile.

"Did you make your bladder gladder on school polyester? Did you syphon the python on a Tiger T-shirt? Tell me the truth! I want the truth!"

Jude slams his brush onto the table. "You want the truth?" he yells. "*You can't handle the truth!*"

It's a line from *A Few Good Men,* which we've seen at least ten times.

And suddenly, in a hangover-induced flash of genius, I get a totally brilliant idea. "Jude," I say, "we need to make a movie."

"Are you out of your freaking mi—"

"We'll make a movie to prove we didn't do it."

When Jude puts his hands on his hips, he looks almost exactly like his mother. "And *how* are we going to do that?"

"We're going to go around asking people questions, on camera. We'll figure out who framed us, and we'll expose them. We'll get Felix Goodwin to help us make it."

Jude looks skeptical. "That sophomore who does all those prank videos? He's cute—I'll give him that. But he's not Oliver Stone." Jude sighs. "Look, Theo, I know it sucks being kicked out of school. But at some point you're just going to have to accept it."

"I have no interest in doing that," I say. "Let's set aside, for one second, the fact that this is probably going to ruin my entire future, and yours, too, if the whole rich-and-famous artist-by-eighteen thing doesn't work out. Don't you think it's weird that we obviously have an enemy? Someone *framed* us. Someone made sure that we got busted for shit we didn't do. We might be going to school with a sociopath."

Jude shrugs. "We're not *going* to school anymore, dummy."

"But what if we could find out who did it? What if we could clear our names? Don't you want that? And what if we could prove Sasha's innocence, too?"

Jude swirls another brush in the turpentine. "I get it now. You're trying to be a knight in shining armor for the crazy-hot girl. That's perfect," he says. He sighs. "Whatever. Fine. When we fail to prove our innocence, *which is exactly what's going to happen,* I'll just submit the video as part of my application to art school. I'll say it's performance art."

It's not exactly the attitude I was looking for, but I figure that for now I've got to take what I can get.

13

I text Sasha and ask her to meet us on Maple Street, between the forbidden zones of Arlington and Five Points Coffee, a few minutes before school lets out. She doesn't text me back, which I try not to worry about. Maybe she's busy ringing up microfiber leggings and jumbo packs of Huggies. Or maybe her dad convinced her that she had better things to do than hang out with a couple of so-called delinquents.

Jude, who's not banned from Five Points for some reason, is sucking down a quadruple-shot iced mocha. He offers me some, but my stomach still can't handle it.

"Is she coming?" he asks me for the fifteenth time.

"It's one of those wait-and-see sort of things," I say.

"I hope you used my line about how it was going to be *The Breakfast Club* meets *Blue's Clues*."

"It's supposed to be a *documentary*," I say for the fifteenth time.

"Right. *The Real Delinquents of Pinewood County*." Then he pokes me in the shoulder. "Look—there he is."

Felix Goodwin's hard to miss. He's pro basketball tall, and he's wearing a neon-orange helmet with a GoPro strapped to the top of it. He's carrying a skateboard and a ratty backpack with crumpled papers trailing out of it.

"He's probably on his way to make a video now," Jude says, awe in his voice. "His last one had, like, 500,000 views."

Felix Goodwin, aka the FBomb, is famous for recreating the internet's best fail videos. Shot for shot, he makes it look like he's slammed his junk on a razor-sharp skateboarding ramp or caught himself on fire after hitting a flaming gourd with a baseball bat—things that real people actually did and then posted online.

In other words, Felix turned his childhood obsession with *America's Funniest Home Videos* into a kind of YouTube empire. This doesn't necessarily make him director material; I can admit that. But he has a jillion followers and good editing software, so he'll be a far better bet than we are when it comes to figuring out how to make this movie.

"Hey, Felix," Jude calls. "Can we talk to you for a second?"

Felix slowly ambles over and then says, in a friendly sort of drawl, "Y'all know my mom told me not to hang out with criminal elements."

I step forward. "You know we're not criminal elements," I say. "Although, actually, that *is* why we're here. Do you remember how I let you copy my geometry homework all last year?"

Felix shrugs. "Still only got a C."

"I'm sorry to hear that, but it's not my fault that you didn't copy it very well," I say. "The thing is, I did that out of the goodness of my heart, and now I'm going to ask you to do something out of the goodness of yours."

"It's right up your alley, too," Jude adds.

Felix looks unconvinced. "Lay it on me," he says.

"We want you to help us make a movie," I say.

He laughs. "Seriously? You want me to film you guys, like, I don't know, reading books or something? Isn't that what y'all are into? Or helping little old ladies cross the street?"

He's cracking himself up, but I ignore it. "Jude and I

were expelled the other day, as you no doubt know. And so was Sasha Ellis, and so was Parker Harris. I don't care about Harris, but the rest of us I do care about. We shouldn't have been kicked out, and we want you to help us prove it."

"Why me?" Felix asks.

"You have better gear, for starters," I say.

"He means that you have a lot of natural directorial talent," Jude interjects.

"Right. Plus you have a channel. If you put something we make on YouTube, a million people are going to see it. And everyone knows that if you want people on your side, you need publicity."

Felix scratches his chin—a funny, old-man gesture. "It's a ballsy move," he says. "That's cool." He shakes his head and smiles. "But I don't think so, man. Dekum and Palmieri are scary, and I gotta keep on their good side, you know?" And he's about to walk away when something stops him.

I don't have to turn around to know just what it is.

The look on Felix's face has changed completely, like he was standing in the pouring rain and suddenly the sun appeared and showered him in warmth and light.

I'm obviously not the only person Sasha has that effect on.

Felix blinks and turns back to me. "She wants to do it, too?"

I nod.

"Jesus," he says.

Sasha's beside me now, her sunglasses pushed up on her head and her eyes on Felix. She says, "Hey, F." Simple as that. Doesn't even use his full name.

"Hey, girl," he says.

"Are we making a movie or what?" she asks.

"I don't know," Felix says, clearly now tormented by indecision.

Sasha puts her hand, ever so briefly, on his forearm. She says, "Why don't we just talk about it a little more? Come out to Theo's place tomorrow after school. Bring a camera."

Felix shakes his head like he just can't believe what he's about to say. "Because I'm a gentleman," he says, "I agree to discuss this tomorrow."

Sasha bestows upon him one of her rare smiles.

And I die inside—just a little—because it isn't meant for me.

14

The next day, as planned, we gather at the Property. Jude, Sasha, and Felix are sitting in a circle on the dock, making small talk and demolishing the supersize bag of Ruffles I picked up at the 7-Eleven. Although Felix looks iffy still, he's brought his brand-new iPhone, some clip mics, and a small, complicated-looking box he tells us is a field production mixer.

Jude's going on about the movie *Tangerine,* which was shot on iPhone 5s's, while Felix extolls the virtues of aerial drone videography and Sasha demands to know if anyone has seen Hitchcock's *Rear Window,* "which is less about creepy voyeurism than it is about the quotidian horror of marriage—I mean, it's about *uxoricide,* for godssakes."

I belatedly realize that I am surrounded by serious AV nerds. Also, I have no idea what *uxoricide* means.

In other words, so far, so good.

It's just about time to call the meeting to order when Parker pulls up in his dad's Escalade, and my mood *plummets*.

I turn to Sasha. "What's he doing here?"

"I told him he should come," Sasha says matter-of-factly. "He was expelled, too, you know."

"Yeah," I say, "because, unlike the rest of us, he deserved to be."

Sasha's either completely unruffled by my annoyance or else she doesn't even notice it. "Well, maybe he deserves to be a part of the movie, too."

"I can't possibly see why."

Jude says, "I can. The camera will love those cheekbones."

Parker's footsteps are heavy on the wooden dock. He must be two hundred if he's a pound. Stopping at our circle, he towers over us like a cliff. "Yo," he says.

"How's Chase Academy?" Jude asks, blinking up at him. "You like those cravats?"

"Fuck off," Parker says, but without malice. He sits down next to Sasha. He's wearing douchebag mirrored sunglasses and the Chase uniform of starched khaki pants and a Wall Street button-down.

Honestly, I feel like driving away in his vile SUV. Maybe running it into a ditch.

"Parker, this is Felix," Sasha says. "Felix, I'm sure you've encountered Parker before."

"Yo," Parker says again.

Jude says, "I'm sure he'll be more eloquent when the camera's on, Felix."

Felix grins. "If he isn't, we can just ask him to crush something. *Hulk...SMASH!*"

"Hulk not think! Hulk crush!" Jude yells.

"I'm right here, gonads," Parker says.

And I no longer have any idea how I'm going to make this plan work. What am I supposed to *do* with these people, half of whom don't even like one another? I knew that trying to make a movie was kind of crazy, but obviously it was stupid, too. I should just let the world keep on thinking that I'm a fuckup.

I start to head to the gazebo. Maybe there's a drop of Knob Creek left. Maybe I can send everyone home and have another one-sided conversation with my dead dad.

"Don't you want to say something, Theo?" Sasha asks.

I turn around and shrug. "I wanted to talk about making a movie that would prove none of us deserved what we got. But the Abominable Bro-man here is *not* innocent, and that screws up my cast!" Then I stop and hold my breath. *Did I just call Parker Harris, star quarterback and the biggest, most jacked junior to ever walk the halls of Arlington, the Abominable Bro-man? To his face? Is today now my last day on earth?*

"Uh-oh," Jude whispers.

Parker starts to stand up, but Sasha holds up a hand and says, "Parker, don't let him get under your skin."

Parker nods. "Ignore the dork. I can do that."

"Except that you have to listen to his idea," Sasha says.

Parker shoots her a look that says *I would sooner rip him limb from limb.*

Jude clears his throat, like he's going to play peacemaker— he *was* the football team mascot, after all, so he's put in his suck-up-to-Parker time.

"Actually, Sasha," I say hurriedly, "why don't *you* explain it?"

Sasha's chilly eyes meet mine. She raises one skeptical, penciled eyebrow. "All right," she says finally. "Fine."

She stands up, and everyone's eyes are instantly on her. She's not nervous; her voice doesn't waver. "We got a raw deal, you guys. We all know that. But we are *not* going to let the Arlington administration determine our fates. We are *not* going to stand for our unfair punishment any longer.

With the help of mighty Felix and his amazing Steadicam, we're going to track down the true perpetrators of these crimes and be exonerated."

Felix flushes and ducks his head. I could've never convinced him to say yes, but a few words from Sasha and his reluctance crumbles. I watch it happening: his shoulders slump and his posture loosens. He may not *want* to say yes, but in his mind he already has.

Then Sasha glances down at her notebook before looking back at all of us. "In the immortal words of Simone de Beauvoir, 'Defending the truth is not something one does out of a sense of duty or to allay guilt complexes, but *is a reward in itself.*' In other words, it doesn't matter if it is a crazy idea. It doesn't matter if it works. We are going to do it anyway."

"But it *will* work!" I yell. "It has to!"

Everyone turns to stare at me, and I can feel my cheeks go hot. I'm not one for public speaking, but since everything else in my life's been turned upside down, I might as well give it a shot. "I don't know about you all," I say, "but I'm not a delinquent, and I'm not ready to be written off. I want *justice*. I want to know how that picture got onto my account and why I'm the one who got saddled with Palmieri's stupid 'banquet of consequences.' I will prove my innocence. I will tell my side of the story. And I will make my own goddamn ending!"

No one says anything for a long time. Then Felix says, "Cut!" and puts down the camera I hadn't even noticed him holding.

"That'll go in the trailer," he says. "If you ask me, it's got Sundance written all over it."

15

"*You're in for real now,*" I say, "aren't you?" I can't keep the giddiness from my voice. *This crazy idea just might work.*

Felix shrugs. "Kinda seems like it."

"That's great," Sasha says. "*You're* great. So what's the next step?"

Felix, all business now, hands her a clip mic. "Put this on. Here, it attaches right to your collar."

She fumbles with it a bit but gets it in the right place eventually, and then she says, "Okay, now what?"

"Now I go to lacrosse practice," Parker says, standing up.

Sasha whirls around. "Wait, Parker," she says. "We

need you," and Parker stops in his tracks like an obedient dog.

I wonder what that's supposed to mean. Who exactly needs him? *I* sure don't. But does she? And as long as I'm questioning Sasha's pronouncements, does she think Felix is so great for agreeing to help us or great in general?

"We're all in this together," Sasha insists. "Every single one of us."

Jude nods emphatically and Parker grunts in what is possibly assent.

Although obviously I'd like it better if Parker took a hike, I say, "Okay, great. Can we start filming?"

Felix nods, fiddling with a knob on his mixer, and Jude says, "Exterior, pond, midafternoon," like he's reading off a screenplay that exists only in his head.

Felix glances up at him. "That'd work—a nice wide-angle shot of the water and the trees," he agrees. "And we could have voiceovers, which'd be you guys."

"Right. We'll want to say who we are and why we're making this movie," I say.

"*In a world,*" Jude says, sounding exactly like that guy who does all the movie trailer voiceovers, "where *justice* is a four-letter word, four *brave teenagers* rise up to—"

"Shut your muffin hole, Tigger," Parker says, and surprisingly, Jude does.

Felix says to Sasha, "You can just go ahead and start talking. Tell us who you are. Say whatever pops into your head."

The sun, glinting on the water, throws diamonds of light onto Sasha's face. She gives her profile to the camera, which is Felix's iPhone 7. Everyone waits, still and silent.

"My name is Sasha Aline Ellis, and I'm seventeen," she begins. "A Scorpio, if anyone cares. A pescatarian. An ex–Girl Scout. A failed flutist. A former equestrian." She smiles fleetingly before her face goes expressionless again. "I guess I used to be a lot of things that I'm not anymore," she says. "I moved here when I was thirteen, and I'm still waiting to move away again. Sartre says that hell is other people, right? Well, he should have seen *this* place. It's like next-level torture. Nothing but PTA moms, soccer dads, and middle-manager zombies, devoid of imagination or soul and malicious toward anyone who *does* have it."

Ouch, I think, but Sasha's not even done yet.

"News flash: we live in a Podunk trash heap, populated by small-minded, TV-drugged villagers obsessed with finger-pointing and judgment," she goes on. "They're too lazy to actually investigate crimes, so they just pin them on whoever's convenient. But we're not all guilty, and we're going to prove it." She turns head-on to the camera and says, "How was that?"

"She's definitely not Switzerland," Jude says to me.

"That was amazing," I tell her. "Though you might want to consider being a *little* more diplomatic toward the PTA moms and the middle managers."

"In that case, you might have to write me a script," Sasha says. "Extemporaneous speech brings out my natural bitterness." Then she bats her eyelashes at me, but sarcastically. I didn't know a person could do that.

"We'll work on it," I say.

She tries to hand the mic to Parker, who looks at it like it's a cockroach, and so she clips it to his shirt. Then Felix poses him on the end of the dock, gazing poetically out at the water. He really is almost obscenely good-looking, which I resent him for.

"Tell us who you are now," Felix says. "Again, just say whatever pops into your head."

Parker sighs. "Fine. My name is Parker Harris. I'm a junior. I hold the state record for passing touchdowns and passing yards in regular season play. I can run a hundred-yard dash in eleven seconds and rep 210 on the bench press forty-five times. My clean and jerk PR is 340."

I'm about to suggest that he cut the stats, but Felix apparently does it for me; he whispers something to Parker, who grunts again and then goes on. "My dad started me playing flag football when I was six. I got the shit kicked out of me regularly by nine-year-olds. Our team was the Volcanoes, and we totally blew. But I started weight lifting when I was twelve..."

My mind wanders as Parker continues to drone on about his athletic prowess. "Are you as bored as I am?" I whisper to Jude.

Jude says, "He's far from a scintillating orator, but he's a very credible romantic lead."

"This is a documentary, remember?" I say, annoyed. "There *is* no romantic lead."

Jude gives me the side-eye. It says *Whatever, Romeo.*

16

I know I said there's no such thing as miracles. But today, when everyone else leaves the Property, Sasha stays behind. As the cars pull away, she walks to the end of the narrow dock and kicks off her sandals. Barefoot, her hair blowing loose around her shoulders, she stares intently at the water.

She was laughing, almost giddy, when we finished up the introductions, but as Felix packed up his equipment, her mood seemed to darken. She didn't even wave good-bye to Parker.

I watch her now, wondering what's going through that wild, baffling mind of hers. I start to take a few steps toward her, but then I stop myself. Maybe she wants to be left alone.

I take a deep breath and look around. Evening's the prettiest part of the day out here. The pond is like blue glass, and the breeze rustles the tips of cattails as the sun starts to lower itself toward the horizon. It's just so damn *peaceful*. Not that I can relax, though, because of Sasha. What does she want? Why did she stay?

Then Sasha turns around, as if she's heard my thoughts. "I don't want to go home."

I smile at her. "I know the feeling," I say. "My mom's never home because she works all the time. So why bother?"

"I sort of have the opposite problem," Sasha says. "My dad—" Then she stops.

"What?"

She shakes her head. "Nothing, never mind. So what do we do now?"

And what *I* say—without even meaning to—is "Do you want to fish?"

Immediately I regret it. What a stupid question! A girl like Sasha Ellis doesn't want to *fish*. And for a second she glances back toward the driveway, like maybe she wishes she'd left with the others.

Then she says, quietly, "Why not?"

And because I don't know what else to do, I get the pole from the shed, and from the garden I pluck a giant night crawler for bait.

"Don't look," I say as I slice off his back half and impale it on the hook.

She does look, though, and it makes her shudder.

"Sorry," I say.

"Don't apologize to *me*," she says.

"Sorry, worm," I say. "But you'll regenerate another tail, so don't worry."

We walk to the end of the long dock, and I set down the tackle box. I cast the line into the center of the pond, and then I hand Sasha the fishing pole. The red-and-white bobber floats in the placid water.

"What am I supposed to do with it?" Sasha asks.

"You just sit and wait, basically. It's kind of boring, I guess. That's why fishing usually involves beer."

The truth is, I love fishing—my dad and I used to do it every weekend—but I don't see how I could explain that to her, not in a way that would make her understand.

She looks skeptically at the pole. "I guess I thought there was more to it."

Out of the corner of my eye I watch her profile. I feel like I should talk more now—or somehow attempt to entertain her—but I'm not Jude, and that kind of thing doesn't come so easily to me. *You need to say something smart, Theo,* I think, and then I hear myself saying, "Well, Hemingway was a fisherman..."

"Yeah, *The Old Man and the Sea*," Sasha says. "I read that one."

I haven't, but I decide not to admit it. "Once, when he was trying to pull in this big marlin, a bunch of sharks started attacking it. So he brought out a submachine gun and shot them all."

"That's horrible," Sasha says.

"Yeah, and it didn't even work, because all that blood just made the surviving sharks go crazy."

She shudders again. "I wouldn't care if I didn't catch anything *ever*."

But even as she says this, the bobber dips down under the water. "Look, you've got something!" I yell.

The pole bends toward the pond, and Sasha struggles to turn the reel.

"It might be big," I say. I can't keep the excitement from my voice.

As the bobber comes closer, the fish bucks and thrashes on the line, pulling it under again. The pole arcs dangerously low. "Keep reeling," I say, "come on!"

"I'm trying," Sasha yells.

The fish splashes wildly by the end of the dock, and I reach down and grab the line with my hands. And then I gasp. "No way—you *caught* him."

Sasha looks worried. "What do you mean?"

Spinning and flopping on the end of the line is the fish my dad used to call Grandpa Bass. He's two feet long and ten pounds at least. "This is the dude my dad tried to catch for *years*."

"How can you tell?" Sasha asks.

I lay him down on the dock and put my foot on his heaving side to hold him still. Besides the hook we caught him with, there are three old fishhooks embedded forever in his gaping mouth. "There," I say. "The evidence."

I don't know whether to be happy that Sasha caught him or sad that my dad and I never did.

I'm leaning toward the second option.

The fish struggles under my foot, and I'm amazed at how strong he is. How full of life. If only my dad were here to see this—he'd cackle with triumph and run to grab a fillet knife. A stab of grief shoots through me as I reach down to pull my hook out of the bass's bony lip.

"Let's eat him," I say, reaching for my own knife in the tackle box. "He'll be good."

Sasha looks at me in horror.

"What?" I ask. "You said you were a pescatarian."

Without a word, she reaches out and *shoves* me. I lose my balance, and my foot slips off the fish. Before I can protest, she's picked him up and flung him back into the water.

She turns to me, eyes blazing. "*That's* where he belongs," she says. "Not on top of a grill."

I watch the ripples he made spread and fade. I'll probably never see that beautiful bass again. "Okay," I say, my voice sounding a little choked. "That's fine. It's not a big deal."

I sit down on the end of the dock then, and she folds herself next to me. We're so close that our arms are almost touching. We drop our feet into the water.

"I'm sorry," she says. "But I'm also not."

"I know," I say. "I take it *your* dad doesn't fish."

"My dad would like the drinking part of it. My dad—" Then Sasha stops and shakes her head. "Never mind."

"What?" I say.

"Nothing. Let's not talk, and especially not about him. Let's just sit here, okay?" Her voice sounds small and tired all of a sudden.

"I'm glad you stayed," I say, *though I still don't know why you did.*

She smiles. Brushes my hand ever so quickly, and then pulls it away. My skin tingles where she touched it. I want to put my arms around her, but I'm paralyzed.

And we sit there—me thinking about Sasha, and Sasha thinking about who knows what—until the sun goes down and the stars come out, one by one by one.

17

The Hamburger Inn's ceiling is brown with grease, and even the air feels slightly…oleaginous. (That is a word from my PSAT vocabulary list, a test I really *studied* for— not that my good score matters at all if I can't clear my name.)

The HI has terrible coffee but great pancakes, and they don't care if you sit there all morning nursing the same mug of brown sludge. Another bonus: the owners don't watch the news and have no idea what Twitter is, so they don't know I'm infamous.

Jude is on his second short stack and his third order of sausage. "So you never told anyone your password, right?"

"I barely told anyone it was my *account*," I say. "So

obviously I didn't give out my password. But it's not just the password thing, remember? Palmieri said that the photo was posted from my school IP address."

"So someone got access to your computer," Jude suggests.

"That's what I thought at first," I say. "But I didn't leave it lying around for people to mess with. Either it was in my backpack or I was taking notes on it." Or, of course, I was using it to post to @ArlingtonConfessions: Pop quiz in pre-calc today #fairwarning #gohomesick.

"Did you ever leave it out when you went to the bathroom?" Jude asks.

I shake my head as I dump more sugar into my mug. I'm trying to make the coffee palatable, but so far it isn't working. "No, never."

"Good, because otherwise this case is impossible." Jude nudges me. "Do you like how I called it a case? I'm going full Sherlock."

"There are basically two possibilities," I say. "Either someone sneaked it out of my backpack and replaced it before I noticed or else someone faked my IP address."

"Both of those sound complicated," Jude says.

"Yeah. So doesn't it seem like someone must have really been pissed at me?"

He shrugs. "Yeah, it kind of does."

"The last tweet I sent was about Tom Thorn getting so wasted that he didn't recognize his own dad."

Jude giggles. "That was a good one."

"So maybe *he* did it. Maybe he wanted to get even," I suggest.

Jude contemplates this for a minute. "He does seem like he could hold a grudge. But he's definitely not the stealthy type. And I was in computer class with him last year, and he can barely turn on a Chromebook."

"Maybe he had help with that," I say.

And I can see it in Jude's eyes: we both think of the exact same person at the exact same time. Jere7my Sharp, misanthropic D&D dungeon master and computer geek extraordinaire.

"I think we'd better go talk to ol' Jeremy," I say.

"Jere-*seven*-my," Jude corrects. "You prep the questions. I'll go get Felix's camera. We'll collar him at lunch."

And with that, Jude vanishes, leaving me with the bill. Luckily the HI's got the cheapest breakfast in town.

18

I text Sasha: Interview #1. Jere7my Sharp. Noon. Merlin's Palace.

She doesn't write me back, but by now I don't expect her to. Either she'll join us or she won't, and there's nothing I can do about it but hope it's the former.

Although Jude fails to separate Felix from his iPhone 7, he does manage to borrow a sweet little Sony minicam he swears he knows how to operate. He takes a test video as we walk toward Merlin's Palace, Pinewood's lone gaming store and unofficial nerd headquarters, which is just a few blocks away from Arlington. Honor roll juniors and seniors are allowed to leave school grounds at lunchtime, and Merlin's attracts Jere7my like a magnet.

I know this because we used to be friends.

Sure enough, he's standing in front of the window, looking at a new Magic: The Gathering deck display. He's small, pale, and slightly undernourished looking. Maybe it's because he spends all his lunch money at Merlin's.

"Do you think his mom still dresses him?" someone whispers in my ear.

I whirl around in surprise. It's Sasha, grinning triumphantly at having snuck up on me.

"Boo," she says and pokes me in the ribs.

I flush. Try not to stammer. "Glad you could join us," I say. "Right there is our first POI."

She raises an eyebrow at me. "Does that mean 'person of interest'? Nice cop vocab, nerd." She looks back at Jere7my. "Oh, my God, I don't know why I called *you* a nerd. His T-shirt says EAT SLEEP CODE!" she says. "Wow. He's such a pure central-casting geek he might as well be wearing a pocket protector and a clip-on bow tie."

This is unkind but sadly accurate. And I happen to know that Jere7my's mom *did* dress him, at least up till age ten, but I won't tell Sasha that.

As we approach, Jude filming, Jere7my turns toward us with a nervous look on his face. "Should I call 911?" he asks.

"Why would you say that?" Sasha asks in a lilting voice.

"In my experience," Jere7my says, "it rarely works out

when a group of people approaches me. It ends in physical pain or social humiliation and oftentimes both."

"Our aim is neither," Sasha says. "I'm Sasha. We've never officially met. You are...Jere-seven-my?"

He refuses to shake her offered hand. "The seven is *silent*," he says.

"Oh," Sasha says, trying very hard to keep a straight face. "Sorry."

I cut to the chase. "So, Jeremy, I've been having problems with my computer."

"Bummer," he says insincerely. "Your porn not downloading fast enough?"

"Very funny. Actually I'm having problems with people making it look like I posted things that I didn't."

Jere7my sniffs. "So you find the closest coder and menace him."

Unconsciously I take a step backward. I basically tower over the poor kid, but I'm so used to being dwarfed by Parker that it never occurred to me that *I* could seem intimidating, too.

And then Sasha, who's definitely more dangerous than I am, moves forward. "Can you tell us how a photograph could be made to look like it came from Theo's computer, Jere-seven-my?" Sasha asks. "Oops, I mean *Jeremy*. If you answer, we'll be nice."

He sighs. He's outnumbered, and he might as well get it over with. "Do you have encryption set up on your router?" he asks me.

"I don't know," I say. "It was at school."

"Wow, menacing *and* ignorant," Jere7my mutters. "Arlington has encryption. So my guess is that someone spoofed your computer's IP address."

"Which means...?" I ask.

"Xerox previous sentence about ignorance," Jere7my says under his breath.

"You're not coming off as a sympathetic character on my video here," Jude points out.

Jere7my's shoulders straighten. "Fine. Okay. Internet protocol specifies each IP packet has to have a header with the address of the sender of the packet, and—"

"But we don't need hacker talk," Jude interrupts.

Jere7my glares at him. "That's not hacker talk. That's basic technical information you should be embarrassed not to know. Anyway, spoofing is when someone fakes their address so it looks like it comes from yours. I don't know why anyone would do that to you."

"To make it look like I sent it, obviously," I say. "Now who's the dense one?"

"Is that something you could do?" Sasha asks Jere7my.

"Do I speak FORTRAN?" he says, with a tone like *Do*

bears shit in the woods? "And C, C plus plus, C sharp, Java, Python, Ruby—"

"Did you help Tom Thorn post the picture to my Twitter?" I demand.

At this, Jere7my starts to laugh. "Please. I have much better things to do with my time. Look, I can't help with your little *investigation*, and I have a Kaladesh deck to purchase."

He tries to shimmy past us, but I stand in front of him and Jude brings the camera in close.

"We used to be friends," I say.

"The operative words being *used to*."

"Yeah, I'm sorry I couldn't follow you down the D&D rabbit hole. Did you do this to me?"

"If I wanted to hurt you, I'd have done a much better job," Jere7my says. "This is toddler stuff."

"What would you have done?" Sasha asks. "Just out of curiosity."

Jere7my smiles. "I could clean out his savings account. I could have him declared legally dead. I could have a hundred thousand people camped on his front lawn in hours by telling them he was giving away Segways. I could have six pounds of heroin sent to his mother at her office."

"Really?" Without a doubt, Sasha sounds impressed.

"Well, the last one might be tricky," Jere7my admits.

He sighs. "Look, I'm not the one to blame for your problems, okay? You'll have to keep looking."

Sasha says, "Who else could do this?"

"I don't know," Jere7my says, scowling. Interestingly, he seems immune to Sasha's charms. "There's no varsity hacking team at Arlington, in case you hadn't noticed."

"You're a lone wolf, huh? Renegade bot guy over here," Sasha says, trying to provoke him.

Jere7my scoffs. "A human is not a bot by definition... oh, never mind."

"Well, when you get tired of being alone, you can help us out," Sasha says.

Jere7my shrugs noncommittally.

"Everyone needs a friend," she says. Then Sasha looks at me and Jude like we're perfect proof of this, and despite this failed interview, my stomach gives a little lurch of happiness.

But Jere7my just flips all of us off, and then he disappears into Merlin's.

19

On Fridays, my mom works only one job instead of two, which means she'll actually be home for dinner. Since this qualifies as a special occasion, I decide to break the frozen burrito cycle and surprise her with food made from an actual recipe. It seems crazy now, but we used to do it all the time, back when there were three of us.

I'm salting the pasta water when I hear her come in. "Oh, my God, what is that fantastic smell?" she calls.

I can hear her taking her shoes off and throwing them into the bin we keep by the door. When she comes into the kitchen, she looks pale and tired, and her bank uniform—blue logo shirt, black pants—is rumpled.

"If that tastes anywhere near as good as it smells, I

might cry from gratitude," she says. She sinks down at the table and lays her head on the worn wood. "Do you need any help? I sort of hope not, because I'm not sure I can stand up again."

"I've got it covered," I say. I made a salad—well, I made a bowl of lettuce with ranch dressing on it—and I even set the table.

"What are you cooking?" she asks.

"Spaghetti carbonara," I say proudly.

"What's that?"

"Dad used to make it, remember? Bacon, egg, and vast quantities of cheese and butter over tagliatelle. He called it the Egg McMuffin of pasta."

My mom sighs. "Oh, God, right. I can't believe I forgot."

I'm not surprised, though. She's forgotten a lot of things since he died, maybe even on purpose—as if amnesia might somehow be protection against grief. And I get it. A lot of days, I try not to think about him at all. Sometimes it even works.

When the pasta's ready, I put our plates down and sit across from her, and for a little while neither of us says anything because we're demolishing our food. It really *is* good.

But eventually my mom looks up at me and shakes her head. "I feel like I haven't seen you in days."

Maybe because you haven't, I think.

"Seriously, you might even be taller. How's it going? How's life?"

I'm not sure how much she really wants to know. "Do you want the long answer or the short?" I ask.

"Up to you," she says, trying to sound cheerful.

I decide to be quick but honest. "I could be better," I say. "I mean, I could still be in school. And I could not be labeled a criminal and a pervert."

And I could still have a dad.

My mom puts down her fork and sighs. "I'm so sorry I wasn't there for you at your hearing. I really can't believe I—"

"I don't know what you could've done," I say quickly. I don't need her to feel worse than she already does. "We thought everything would turn out all right."

"Yes, we did, didn't we?"

"I don't know why, though, considering what our luck has been lately." I can't keep the bitterness from my voice. "We should have had a clue, you know? Things haven't really been working out for us."

My mom sits back. She takes a deep breath and wipes a lone tear from her cheek. "I know. Honestly, I feel like I'm drowning, Theo," she says mournfully. "Every day when I open my eyes, all I want to do is close them again. I don't know what to do. I'm furious at your father, and I miss him with all my heart." She shakes her head. "This isn't what my life was supposed to be like. And more importantly, it's not what your life was supposed to be like."

"No, not ideally," I agree.

"But we still have each other, right?" she asks.

Sort of, I think. "Yeah," I say.

"I just want you to be happy," she says.

"That's maybe easier said than done right now," I say. "But I want you to know that I'm going to make things better."

"Are you going to win the lottery?" she asks, trying to smile. "Because it would be really helpful if you could do that."

"I read somewhere that statistically I'm more likely to become a saint," I say. "Also, I'm not old enough to buy a lottery ticket. But I *am* going to prove that I had nothing to do with that picture. And when I do, I won't fail junior year. I'll get a scholarship to college. And—"

"And *then* you'll become a saint, plus a doctor or a lawyer who can support me in my old age," she says, smiling.

"Right," I say. "Innocence, then canonization, then law school."

"You're amazing, Theo," my mom says.

I know she means it. But her voice just sounds so tired, so unconvinced.

20

An hour later, my mom's already fallen asleep in front of *Cosmos;* Neil deGrasse Tyson intoning about how we're all made of star stuff can't compete with a seventy-hour workweek. I write a note telling her that I'm borrowing the minivan, and then I head over to Jude's house.

"We're going on a field trip," I tell him.

"Should I bring the camera?" he asks, already putting on his shoes.

I shake my head. "This is on the DL."

"On the DL on the reals?" Jude says, making fun of my old-school slang. "Hey, don't punch me again!"

"Poke," I correct him.

"Where are we going?" he asks, buckling into the front seat.

"You'll see."

Five minutes later, we're pulling up in front of Sasha's big fancy house. And though I basically prayed the entire drive over that her dad wouldn't be home, he's the one who opens the door.

"Good evening," he says to me. His voice is polite but cold, and I detect its mocking undertone. His eyes shift to Jude. "Hello there, new youngster. Tell me, are you also a delinquent? Inquiring minds want to know."

"Yes, sir," Jude says brightly. "I mean, accused but not actually guilty. Just like your daughter, sir."

Professor Ellis raises a skeptical eyebrow. "Good habits formed in youth make all the difference," he says. "Aristotle said that. And you, being the young, bipedal mammals that you are—proto-men, shall we say?—would do well to keep that in mind."

I don't really know what he's talking about, and Sasha, who has appeared behind him in the hall, rolls her eyes at his back.

"Do you want to go to the game with us?" I call.

Both Sasha and Jude look at me like I've gone insane.

"The *baseball* game?" Jude asks. "At *school?*"

"Why in the world would we want to do that?" Sasha says.

"Because I feel like experiencing an all-American pastime," I say. Though honestly, I never had any interest in going to a game until it was forbidden for me to do so.

Professor Ellis turns to his daughter. "I don't think you've been to a high school sporting event before."

"Yeah," she says, "and that was on purpose."

"You should probably keep it that way," he says. "Good evening," he says to us, and he starts to close the door.

But Jude holds out his arm to stop it. "Don't knock it till you try it, honey."

Sasha gives him a funny look. Then she looks at her dad. She straightens her shoulders. "Fuck it," she says, grabbing a sweater and water bottle before slipping past her father. "Let's go."

"Watch your language," Professor Ellis says. He catches her arm as she goes by. "And don't be out too late," he adds gruffly.

"Don't worry," she says, shaking him off, and then she starts running to the car, yelling "Shotgun!"

Her dad stands backlit and imposing in the doorway, watching us go.

"Thanks," Sasha says once they're all buckled in.

"For what?"

"Thinking of me tonight."

I almost laugh then, because she has no idea how much I think about her.

I doubt that Palmieri, Dekum, or any of their minions would recognize my mom's Honda minivan, but I park a few blocks from the field anyway. It's twilight, and the big floodlights are blazing. Arlington's baseball team is number three in the state, so the stands are packed.

We slip in through a side gate as the announcer calls the names of the players. They jog onto the field, waving at their fans like they've already won.

"I should be out there, too," Jude says wistfully. "Before the national anthem, I always did my special little shimmy dance."

"Well, tonight you're below the stands with your delinquent friends," I say, pulling him along until we're all hidden underneath the aluminum bleachers. "And lucky for you, I brought snacks."

Jude snatches the bag of Kettle chips out of my hand as the opposing team makes the first pitch. We watch as Jonas Adair, a senior, slams the ball into right field and makes it all the way to third base. The next batter brings Jonas home and gets himself to second. By the time the first inning is over, we've got six runs to the other team's zero. Above us, the crowd stomps their feet, cheers, and throws popcorn into the air, which falls down on us like snow.

I can't help feeling excited, too, but whether it's about our team's near-guaranteed victory or my trespassing with my friends I can't be sure. Probably it's the latter, though, because the fact that I could even *consider* calling Sasha Ellis a friend is still mind-boggling to me. I watch her as she takes a swig from her water bottle and then grabs a handful of chips. In the shadows, her pale skin almost seems to glow.

Then, over by the concession stand, directly in my line of sight, I spot Palmieri. For a second, I stop breathing. He orders a popcorn—he doesn't pay for it, I notice—and when he gets the big tub, instead of returning to the bleachers, he just keeps standing there, tossing kernels into his mouth by the handful.

I tell myself that it's dark under here. There's no way he can see us.

"I wouldn't have pegged you for a sports fan," Sasha's saying to Jude. "I thought you just liked dressing up in tiger drag."

Jude says, "Yeah, the costume's my favorite part, I'm not ashamed to admit it. But it's my job to be enthusiastic about Arlington athletic endeavors."

By this point, our team's up by so many runs that the coach puts in our worst players. The bases are loaded when

Simon Ripley, a sophomore who's eighty pounds soaking wet, steps up to the plate. The pitcher fires a fastball. And by some crazy miracle—yes, it would seem that they *are* possible—Simon hits a freaking *homer*.

Jude lets out an ear-piercing shriek of happiness, and Sasha gives a little leap of excitement, and we're all clapping and hollering while Simon gets over his shock and starts to run. And that's when Palmieri hears the racket we're making from our hiding place. He tosses his popcorn on the concession stand counter and ducks under the bleachers to investigate. "Who's there?" he calls.

For a split second, our eyes lock in the dimness. Sasha and Jude freeze. Then all three of us are running away from him, scrambling through the obstacle course of bleacher supports, empty popcorn cartons, and discarded Big Gulps.

Palmieri shouts, "Hey, you! Stop right there!" and Sasha cackles as she sprints beside me. She's so fast she pulls ahead, but then she turns around, pausing for an instant, to flip our assistant principal off.

My breath is loud in my ears as we blast out from underneath the bleachers and instinctively scatter, as if fleeing punishment is second nature to us. My feet pound on the pavement of the parking lot. I don't know where Sasha and Jude are now, but I hear loud breathing behind me.

Palmieri.

I speed up, my lungs burning. I've got four hundred yards before I'm off school property, and then Palmieri can't touch me. I can't look, but I know he's right behind me, seconds from collaring me. I can practically smell his cologne.

I'm gasping for breath, and any second my lungs are going to explode. *Just a few more yards.* In a final burst of effort, I reach the sidewalk on the edge of school property, and in three more strides I'm in the middle of the road, and then suddenly I'm crashing through a stand of evergreens and collapsing in their cool darkness, my fall broken by a thick carpet of pine needles.

Flat on my back, I suck in air in heaving gasps. I can't see Palmieri through the trees, and I have no idea where he is. I try to slow my breath so I can listen for him. Is he waiting for me out there?

For several minutes, nothing happens. Then for several more: silence. I can't believe it—I've actually *escaped.* The adrenaline that was coursing through me slowly dissipates. My breathing's finally returning to normal. I'm about to stand up and hazard a peek out into the street when a figure comes crashing through the branches.

I scramble to get up, desperate to run, but the figure tackles me and knocks all the air out of my lungs. "Gotcha!"

Sasha's breath is warm in my ear, and her laughter sounds like bells.

21

My shirt clings to my sweaty back, my legs are Jell-O, and I feel more alive than I have in months. I let out a whoop of victory, and Jude claps me on the shoulder.

"That, my friend, was amazenards," he says. "What do you think—better than amazeballs? I really hate that term."

"Definitely not better," I say, laughing.

"Amazenuts," Jude says contemplatively. "Amazebollocks. Amazetestes?"

"Oh, my God, shut up," Sasha begs.

The three of us are walking down the middle of an empty, lamplit street. My mom's minivan abandoned at the scene of the crime. Our shadows on the asphalt are so tall that we look like giants. We *feel* like giants: we trespassed and we weren't caught. We raced the AP and *won*.

"I can't believe I thought going to a baseball game would be boring," Sasha says. She's drinking a bomber of Michelob Ultra she bummed off a guy coming out of the 7-Eleven. He was seventy-five if he was a day, and he wouldn't give me and Jude one because we weren't beautiful girls. He actually *said* that.

Not that I care. I'm iffy on alcohol since my date with Knob Creek, and anyway, walking next to Sasha, my hand sometimes brushing against hers . . . it's almost more than I can handle already.

"I just wish you could have seen my mascot dances," Jude says to her.

"Do one now," I say, stopping in the street. "Right here."

Jude shakes his head. "No, I have a different idea. Hang on."

Then he darts away, down the alley between the sub shop and the empty storefront that used to be a record store.

"You gonna pee on someone else's property for real this time?" I call.

Sasha elbows me. "When your friend *furtively rushes down a dark alley,* you don't draw attention to him, genius. He probably *does* need to piss."

"Look around—do you see anyone? Everybody's in their

living rooms, drooling in front of their sixty-four-inch TVs. If Palmieri can't catch us, no one can," I insist.

"Tell that to the police who want to slap him with indecent exposure," Sasha replies.

Jude hisses from the darkness. "I'm not pissing!"

Sasha and I look at each other, shrug, and then duck down the alley in time to see Jude reach into his backpack and pull out a can of spray paint.

"Wait a second—" I say. "You're not—"

Jude looks at me, eyes blazing and defiant. "Basquiat started his career as a graffiti artist. When I'm famous, this Dumpster will be worth millions."

And with that very bold, very possibly deluded statement, Jude starts painting. Sasha and I watch, dumbstruck, as he draws a cartoonish, androgynous face with spiraling eyes and a star exploding behind it. He pulls out another can and draws slashes of red all around it. It's violent and beautiful. I don't know if it's art, but it's definitely not just petty vandalism.

"Jude, we have to go," Sasha says urgently. "I hear someone coming."

"Art is not a crime," he insists.

But then we *all* hear the footsteps, and so we run away like it is. When we stop, lungs aching all over again, Sasha leans over to catch her breath and says, "Fuck this place."

Jude says, "What?"

Sasha stands up and throws her head back. "Fuck this lame-ass town and everyone in it! Fuck everyone but us! 'Hell is empty and all the devils are here!'" She turns to us. "I know you don't like me to explain my references, but that's Shakespeare, *The Tempest,* you dipshits."

Jude shoots me a look that says *What's with the sudden mood shift?*

"Sasha?" I say hesitantly.

She whirls to face me. "If that stupid picture on your lame-ass secret Twitter is basically the most scandalous thing to ever happen in Pinewood, this town suffers from a serious lack of imagination!" she yells. "They have no idea what real crimes are. Some might be going on right under their noses!"

"Have you gone...temporarily insane?" Jude asks politely.

"We should tag more things. We should slash tires. Break shit. Smash the windows! Smash the patriarchy!" In the half-light, Sasha's eyes look like the pinwheels Jude put in his graffiti, and I feel like maybe he was right to question her sanity. She's gone wild and weird all of a sudden, with a nervous bouncing energy. Jude reaches for her water bottle and takes a sniff. He makes a face, then tips it up and drinks.

Then he spits onto the ground. "Warm vodka?" he practically hollers. "That's disgusting!"

"Don't be such an aesthete," Sasha says.

"I don't even know what that word means," Jude says.

"At least you know what a cravat is," I point out.

"The point isn't how it *tastes,* you idiots. It's how it makes you feel." Sasha holds her arms out and starts to spin around. Her dark hair flies around her head, and she looks like the girl in the scandalous picture—albeit with a shirt on.

Then she stops abruptly and stares at us like she's surprised to see us. Like we've just shown up on this random street in the middle of the night and she doesn't know why we're here. Or why, for that matter, she is.

"Are you okay?" I ask quietly.

Sasha cocks her head at me and squints. "Am I okay? No, I am not okay. I am a lot of other words and none of them is 'okay.' Okay isn't even something I'm interested in being. Okay is boring as shit. I am..." She stops.

She is *what?* I'm dying to know. Her wild eyes pass from me to Jude and back again.

"I'm *tired,*" she says finally. "This stupid town, this ridiculous punishment, this wandering around in the middle of the night because we have nothing better to do with our lives. Do you understand how pitiful this is? We are *wastes of oxygen.* Forget what I said about the patriarchy and the tires. My dad's probably passed out by now, which means it's time for me to go home." And then she turns around and starts walking away.

I'm about to follow her, but Jude stops me. "Her house is, like, six blocks away. Just let her go."

So I stand there, feeling helpless and confused but most of all *abandoned,* as Sasha disappears into the night.

22

It's 11 a.m. a couple of days later and the sun's already blazing across the Property. Jude sits shirtless in the shade of the gazebo, thumbing through an *Us Weekly,* while I wrestle with a replacement board for a railing that's gotten dry rot.

This is the kind of repair I used to do with my dad on Saturdays: we'd walk around the whole Property, checking on everything from the floating dock to the pole-bean trellises and noting what needed fixing. It didn't seem particularly fun back then, but now, of course, I miss it. Miss *him.* Miss every single thing about the life that used to be mine.

Considering I don't know how much longer the Property will belong to us, I'm not sure it makes sense to put my sweat into repairing the deck. I guess I'm doing it because I'm trying to keep my mind off Sasha.

I was hoping she would meet us here, but she still hasn't shown up. She hasn't answered any texts since Friday night, and her phone goes straight to voicemail. Jude tried to assure me that Sasha was just sleeping off a killer hangover, but after a weekend of not hearing from her, I can't shake the feeling that something is wrong. She was acting so strange that night.

Jude puts his magazine down and strolls over, yawning. "Did you know that Damien Hirst is worth over a billion dollars?" he asks.

"As long as you're here, hold that end of the two-by-four steady, right on top of the post. Who's Damien Hirst?"

Jude grabs onto the wood, and I position the nail and start pounding.

"He's the world's richest artist, and he's a former juvenile delinquent," Jude says over the beat of my hammer. "He was a shoplifter, for one, *and* he was accused of check fraud. He had an actual criminal record!"

"Don't get any ideas," I say. "Your painting Friday night was criminal enough."

"I'm just pointing out that if our movie doesn't work out, there's still hope for me," Jude says. "Some people think bad behavior's sexy."

I hit the nail one last time; the head's now flush and the board's in place. "Look," I say, hooking the claw of the hammer into one of my belt loops and letting it hang there. "The movie *will* work out, okay? In fact, this afternoon we're going to interview our next person of interest."

"Who?"

"Palmieri."

Jude gasps. "Are you crazy? He practically tackled us at the baseball game. I do *not* want to go have a little chat with him after that near-death experience."

"It was dark, Jude, and he could barely see us. He could never prove we were there. All he can say is that he chased three kids off school property. We could have been anyone. For all he knows, we were kids from the other school, trying to sabotage team spirit from below."

Jude considers this. "Plausible deniability," he says eventually. "Okay. Maybe. But the guy scares the shit out of me. His biceps are as big as grapefruits."

"We're not going to fight him," I counter. "We're going to ask him a few questions. Like why he assumed we were guilty and never actually investigated the case."

"And how many biceps curls he does every morning," Jude adds.

"Very funny." I grab another nail and get ready to pound it in. "Do you really think Sasha's okay?"

"No, I don't," Jude says. "She's not 'okay,' remember? She thinks okay is stupid and boring. But I promise you that she's fine. She slept in her canopy bed all weekend, dreaming the dreams of the brilliant and half insane."

I nod. "Yeah, you're right. Nothing bad could've happened to her in six blocks. Especially since you and me are still the town's most wanted men."

"Damn straight," Jude says proudly.

"But you don't think we should go to her house?" I ask.

"I'd actually rather face Palmieri than Professor Ellis," Jude says. "'Oh, are you boys criminals? Isn't that just *darling.* Let me sip my Scottish whiskey while I eviscerate you with my rapier wit and my cold, hard eyes, you sniveling, pathetic excuses for adolescent Homo sapiens.'"

I can't help but laugh. "Sasha came by her scorn naturally, I guess," I say.

"But what about the crazy?" Jude asks drily.

"Yeah, where *did* that come from?"

Jude shakes his head. "Who knows? Like I've said a thousand times, Sasha Ellis is a mystery you may never solve."

I want to, though. I want to know Sasha's secrets almost as much as I want to know who set us up and got us expelled.

23

School ended an hour ago, but the grounds are still crawling with kids: the baseball team's practicing bunts on the field while the JV softball girls jog the perimeter, ponytails swinging. Even the drama club's outside for some reason, rehearsing a number from *Annie Get Your Gun* in the parking lot.

Jude, Felix, and I are across the street, watching all the action, and I'd be lying if I said I didn't feel left out—even if I'd rather hand-wash Parker's Jockey shorts than play a sport or sing in a school musical. I just really miss being *part of things.*

"What'd Harper lecture about in English today?" I ask Felix.

He shrugs. "That's my napping period."

"Really?" I say, disappointed. "But that's your easy A."

"It's right after lunch," Felix explains. "Digestion is hard work."

"Guys," Jude says. "Can we just get this over with?" He looks jittery and over-caffeinated, not to mention highly reluctant to be here.

And right then I see Palmieri coming out of the school. "Okay, let's go! Felix, is the camera on?"

"Yeah," Felix says, "but who—"

"Come on, hurry," I say, crossing the street and motioning for them to follow. I hadn't told Felix who we'd be interviewing. If I had, there's no way he would've come. "Mr. Palmieri! Mr. Palmieri!"

"Oh, shit," I hear Felix say. "Dude, this is *not* cool."

Palmieri turns at the sound of his name, and when he sees us, his face darkens. "If you don't get off school property immediately, we're going to have a very big problem," he says.

"I just need to ask you a few questions," I say. My words come out in a tumbling rush. My heart's thudding in my chest, and really, I just want to run away from him again. But I make myself stand my ground. "Why did you *unfairly expel* us? That's my first one."

Palmieri doesn't look remotely remorseful. "Principal

Dekum established a zero tolerance discipline policy this year, and you boys knew that. You were hardly the first to be expelled." Then he looks right at Felix and adds, "And for all I know, you won't be the last, either."

I can hear Felix mutter something under his breath, but he keeps on filming.

"Andy Marcus was caught defecating on the bathroom floor," I say. "So I'm *pretty* sure he deserved to be expelled. And Terry Raines had his little bowie knife show-and-tell in the cafeteria, so that was an obvious call, too. But Jude and I here—you didn't have hard evidence against us!"

Palmieri doesn't even blink. "Circumstantial evidence is all we needed, Mr. Foster. The only *reasonable* conclusion, *supported by the circumstantial evidence,* was that you and your friend were guilty."

"But we didn't get the chance to prove we weren't!"

"You had a hearing," he points out.

"Did you *want* us to get expelled?" I practically yell. "Were you hoping to make an example of us?"

"Don't be ridiculous," Palmieri says, trying to step around Felix to get to his car.

"Or maybe your problem's not with us but with Dekum," I say, desperate to keep Palmieri talking. "I've heard that his new discipline policy isn't so popular. And if people don't like him anymore, what does that mean for you? Do you want to get your boss fired—is that it? Then maybe you can take his place?"

Palmieri shakes his head in disgust. He holds up his hand, like he can block the sound of my voice.

"Or maybe the problem's just with you! You think we're a bunch of degenerates, just because we're not jocks like you used to be?"

He unlocks the door of his stupid Mustang and opens it. But I can't let him go without some kind of reaction.

"Do you like the sense of power that ruining people's lives gives you?" I yell.

Palmieri takes a step toward me, and I suddenly realize how *big* he is. He's like Parker-size, and he's hella pissed. "You should be doing something *productive* with your time," he says, his voice cold and nasty. "Not playing like you're *Vice* magazine reporters with your hipster T-shirts and stupid little microphones. Not sniveling around crying 'Unfair!' And definitely not accusing me of a crime when *you're* clearly the guilty ones. Don't make things any worse for yourselves, boys. And don't make it worse for other people, either." He looks again at Felix. "Choose your friends wisely, Mr. Goodwin. Their habits tend to rub off on you."

Felix starts to back away, but he's still holding the camera up.

"Now get off school property before I call the police."
Palmieri gets into his car and shuts the door.

I turn away in defeat. What had I hoped to accomplish?
Suddenly I don't even know anymore.

"I guess we'd better go," Jude says quietly.

I'm trudging back to Zelda when I feel a hand on my
shoulder. I turn around—it's Palmieri.

"Look," he says gruffly. "I'm not out to get you kids,
and I never was. Like I said, the evidence was against you.
That's not going to change, and I'm sorry. For everything
that happened." He shakes his head then, like he's actually almost sad about it, and he starts to walk away. But a
second later, he turns back. "And remember what I said to
Felix about choosing friends?" he adds. "The same applies
to you, Theo. Be careful around Sasha Ellis."

"*What the hell is that supposed* to mean?" I ask after Palmieri drives away.

"I don't care what it means," Felix says, tucking his camera inside its case. "All I care about is not following y'all down Delinquent Road."

"Being expelled's not so bad," Jude says unconvincingly.

Felix snorts. "Expelled? That's nothing. I'd be dead, because my mom would've killed me."

"Your mom's on the PTA," Jude says. "She hardly seems like a killer."

Felix says, "Looks can be deceiving. Sorry, man, I just don't think this is my fight."

"We're not asking you to be on our side," I say. "We're asking you to *film* our side. It's different."

"It doesn't feel different when Palmieri glares at me like that," Felix says. "Look, you can borrow the minicam. But I don't think I can help you. I've got to get back to my area of expertise. Have you seen the video where the guy tries a parkour flip off a gravestone and then just *bites* it? It's a complete face-plant—he must have knocked out every single tooth in his mouth."

"But Felix—"

"I saw a fake headstone at Boom-Boom's Balloons. Five bucks. It'd be so easy."

I try again. "Felix, we need—"

"Or I could put on a wig and be that chick who was twerking on a moving car. Did you see that? Spoiler alert: she fell the hell off," Felix says.

"The possibilities are endless," Jude agrees glumly.

While Felix goes on listing all the other videos he wants to make, I think about Palmieri and what he said about the evidence against us. I hate to admit that we *do* look pretty guilty.

I also hate to admit that maybe he isn't as big of a dick as I thought he was. I mean, he *apologized*.

So apparently Palmieri's not my enemy. And it doesn't

seem like Jere7my is, either. So who, exactly, was out to get poor Theo Foster?

And then, all of a sudden, I wonder how I could've been so stupid. So focused on myself. The only expelled person who was truly and inarguably guilty? *Parker Harris.*

I grab Jude's arm. "You guys," I say. "We've been going about this all wrong."

"That's what I'm telling you," Felix says. "Theo, you just gotta write a nice op-ed for the school newspaper explaining the truth. You have a real way with words. You don't need me. You don't need a documentary movie."

"That's not what I meant by wrong," I say. "What I meant was: maybe *I'm* not the one with the enemy."

Jude's eyes open wide. "Wait—you think I've got one?"

"No," I say. "I think Parker Harris does."

Jude's eyes go even wider. "No way," he whispers.

"I think someone wanted to get even with the football star," I say, "and you and I are just collateral damage."

25

"*But Parker's basically the king of* the school," Jude says. "Or was."

"Right," I say, "but a king *always* has saboteurs in his ranks."

"*Et tu, Brute?*" Jude mimes being stabbed in the back.

"I really don't know what you two are talking about," Felix says, slinging his backpack over his shoulder. "I mean, it's dramatic and everything, but I gotta jet."

"No, wait," I say, "just come with us to talk to Sasha."

"Sasha?" Felix repeats hopefully. The mere mention of her name changes things for him, it's obvious.

I can sympathize.

"Why do you want to talk to her?" Jude asks. "Isn't Parker your next person of interest?"

"I think we should come at him from an angle," I say. "Plus I want to run my theory by Sasha." *And I want to see her—to make sure she's okay.*

Felix is still reluctant, but the prospect of talking to Sasha, plus our promise to buy him as many Doritos Locos Taco Supremes as he can eat, gets him into the car. He barely fits in Zelda's front seat, and I basically have to origami myself into the back.

When we get to Matheson's, I don't bother to pretend like I'm there to shop. I go straight to Sasha's lane, blindly grab a pack of gum, and slap it down on the conveyor belt.

"There's been a break in the case," Jude blurts before I can say anything.

I elbow him and he yelps.

"We've been asking the wrong questions," I say. "It isn't about who's out to get me. It's about who's out to get Parker."

Sasha's eyes are cold. "This is information you could have sent me in a text," she says.

"That's true," I say, "but maybe I got sick of sending you texts that you never respond to. Maybe I just wanted to look at you and *tell* you what I figured out. Someone wanted to get *Parker* in trouble. He was the one with the most to lose! Did you ever talk to him about that?"

She gives a minute shake of the head. "Parker and I don't do a lot of talking. We never did."

What did *you do?* is something that a deep, dark part of me wants to ask. But I push all thoughts of the two of them together, in *any* way, out of my mind.

"Have you seen him lately?" I ask.

"No," she says. "And you're acting weird."

"I'm not weird, I'm excited."

She picks up my gum, scans it. "You realize that this is absolutely, positively the most disgusting flavor of Trident Layers ever made," she says, dropping it scornfully into a tiny bag.

"I'm not going to chew it. It's just buying a place in line." I hand her the quarters I swiped from my mom's change jar.

"I'll take it," Jude says. "Green apple and pineapple? Sounds delicious."

Sasha says, "You really should go."

"Are these dudes crazy?" Felix asks her. "Are we wasting our time?"

"I don't know," Sasha says. "Maybe you're on the right track. I'm sure plenty of people resent Parker—he's a star quarterback, and everyone knows that quarterbacks are basically megalomaniacal, hypercompetitive, fist-pumping 'roid ragers. But Theo seems to have forgotten that this incredibly thrilling 'break in the case' doesn't help *me* any." She turns to me, and her eyes are as icy as I've ever seen them. "Did you even remember we were supposed to figure out who took all that money?"

I inhale sharply. Sasha's right. I totally forgot. "I'm so sorry," I say. "I just—"

"Don't worry about it," she snaps. "I never asked you to solve my problems."

"But I want to," I say.

"Seriously, you just have to go. You bought your gum. There's the exit."

"Jude," I say, "buy something. Quick."

Jude grabs another pack of gum and puts it on the belt. "Now we have two different Trident flavors to try," he says brightly.

Sasha rolls her eyes. She scans the gum and holds out her hand for Jude's crumpled dollar bill.

"I'm really sorry," I say again. "I just wanted to know if you could think of someone in particular who might have a beef with Parker."

Then Jude says, "Dude, he's here."

I look up, expecting to see the jock himself, here to flirt with Sasha on her break or something. But instead of spotting Parker Harris looming by the front doors, I see Jere7my Sharp. Our eyes meet over the rows of shopping carts, and Jere7my promptly whirls around and goes back outside.

"What the hell?" I say.

"What's your problem *now?*" Sasha asks.

And I don't know why this question bothers me so much. Maybe it's the condescending tone in her voice—like I'm a guy who's always got a bunch of inconsequential problems to whine about, when in fact I'm a guy who has only *one,* very *consequential* problem to deal with.

"What's *your* problem?" I practically yell. "Would it kill you to be friendly for more than ten seconds at a time?"

We stare each other, and I immediately want to take my words back. But I don't, because the look on her face is so scornful that it feels like a knife is being driven into my ribs.

"This gum is actually really good," Jude says, trying to break the icy tension. "I think I'll buy another pack." He puts it down and digs out another dollar from his pants.

Sasha practically hisses like a cat. "Just *take* it, and get the hell out of here."

26

The moon's barely a sliver when I slip out the back door. I can't sleep, and so I just start walking. It's a habit that started in the insomniac months after my dad died; when pacing my room got old, I'd go walk around the dark neighborhoods. It didn't make me feel better, but it gave me something to do.

It's ironic, or depressing, or both, that if my dad were still alive, walking around might've been impossible for him by now. Maybe he'd have been in a wheelchair. Maybe he'd even have had a catheter and a feeding tube.

There's no way of knowing how the disease would have progressed. A lot of people die within a year of being diagnosed. Some—not many—make it to five years. The point is, there was no good ending to that story. There was only a quick one or a slow one.

It's hard to say which would've been worse.

The night air smells like flowers. I swear there's an ordinance in Pinewood that says every yard has to have at least one rosebush, and preferably more like eight. Sasha would claim these roses are yet another example of Pinewood's lack of imagination, but I think they're pretty.

Why on earth did I think I practically *loved* her when actually I barely *know* her? Sasha was always surprising me, and probably only half of the surprises were good ones.

I pass by the 7-Eleven, which at this hour of the night is Pinewood's only hint of life. Its windows are cluttered with posters advertising sales on beef jerky, Big Gulps, and Little Debbie snacks. But then I see a smaller sign that makes me stop in my tracks.

Maybe obsessing over who got me expelled is just too crazy. Maybe I should just accept my fate. Wasn't that a lesson to take from my dad: if you can't win, *quit?*

If I stopped trying to make this idiotic movie, then I'd have a lot more time on my hands. Time I could use to be actually helpful to someone. Like my mom.

I have this fleeting hope that maybe I *can* make everything better, just not in the way I wanted.

I take a deep breath, enter the cold, bright store, and walk up to the register.

"Help you?" the woman asks flatly.

"I'd like to fill out an application," I say.

She raises an eyebrow. "Didn't know we were hiring," she says.

"There's a sign in the window," I say. "Right beneath the one that says you're having a sale on Skoal."

Wordlessly she shoves a piece of paper across the counter to me.

"Do you have a pen?" I ask.

She points to a cup of them, and I reach for one.

"That's ninety-nine cents," she says.

"You mean I need to buy it to use it?" I ask.

"You need to buy a bag of Lay's if you want a potato chip, don't you?"

"But I just want to borrow—"

"Ninety-nine cents," she says again.

I slap a dollar on the counter and pick out a pen, and I fill out the application as quickly as I can. I can feel the woman's eyes on me, and I don't like it. She lifts her Big Gulp and takes a noisy sip.

"Here you go," I say when I'm done. "I'm available anytime for an interview."

She takes the paper, folds it neatly, and while I'm still

watching, she drops it into the trash can. "I know who you are," she says. "We don't need your help."

I'm so stunned by her cruelty that I don't know what to say.

As soon as I hit the parking lot, I start to run. I have no idea where I'm going; I just know that I can't be here.

I thought the worst thing that could happen now was that I'd be stuck in Pinewood, getting my GED and working at the 7-Eleven—that was going to be my rock bottom. But then the *7-Eleven doesn't even want me.* If it weren't so awful, it'd be funny.

I run for at least a mile before I stop. And when I look up, I see I'm on Sasha's street.

Slowly now, panting a little, I walk toward her house. All the lights are on inside, and they throw golden squares onto the dark lawn. Her dad walks into the frame of the dining room window and stops, his back to me. His shoulders are moving, like he's talking. Maybe he's drunk. Maybe he's reciting poetry again.

Sasha might be in the room, too, rolling her eyes at him the way she did that first night I went to her house. Or maybe she secretly likes his recitations and likes having a professor for a dad, even if he acts like a pretentious dick. I'll probably never know the truth.

I look around me in the darkness. Sasha's yard is rose-less, but her neighbor's yard has masses of towering, fragrant bushes. And even though it lacks imagination, I pick six beautiful yellow blooms, and I lay them in a bundle on her front step—an apology for how I acted at Matheson's.

A few weeks ago I would have felt awful about stealing someone's roses. But, as we've already established, *shit changes.*

It's *7:00 a.m. and I need* coffee like I've never needed anything before. Too bad there's not a single bean left in the house—there's just a note from my mom:

> *Drank the last French roast and ate the last granola bar. Sorry, I swear I'll get to the store today!*

I send Jude an SOS text, and a little while later, he rattles up in Zelda. "I must love you very much to get out of bed this early," he says, shaking his head.

"I'm texting Felix, too," I say. "Coffee first, then our next interview." Last night taught me that if I don't prove my innocence, I *really* don't have much of a future—here or anywhere.

"Oh, goody, I can't wait," Jude says. "That last one went so well."

"No sarcasm until after I'm caffeinated."

We drive to Five Points, and Jude goes inside while I loiter near a rusting bike rack. It's a cool, cloudy morning, and I can see, from across the intersection, my former classmates heading into school. It feels like months since I was there, too, walking alongside them.

Someone brushes past me on the sidewalk, and I look up to see Todd Wittig, who used to sit next to me in pre-calc.

"Hey, Todd," I call, but he doesn't turn around. His shoulders hunch and he starts walking faster toward school. "Really?" I hear myself yelling after him. *"Really?"*

His arm lifts then, in what might be a half wave—or not. It might mean *Piss off.*

I never thought expulsion would turn me into such an outcast. If I'd really considered it—which obviously I hadn't—I might've guessed it'd make me just a little bit *cool.* Dropping out of school meant you were a loser, but getting kicked out meant you were a rebel. Shouldn't that be kind of intriguing to people?

Apparently not.

I glance inside the coffee shop. Jude's in line right ahead

of Jenna Tucker and Lulu Trinh, who are unsurprisingly ignoring him.

Then Felix rolls up on his skateboard and stops, popping it up into his hand. "You guys just don't quit, do you?" he says.

"We can't afford to," I say. "And we really need you."

Felix sighs. "Make it quick. I don't want to be late."

"I had an idea last night. What about Parker's ex, Hailey? He broke up with her on Snapchat, and the whole school found out about it. That's humiliating."

"That's definitely cold," Felix says. "But she seems like a nice girl. Not exactly the vindictive type."

Jude appears with my quadruple-shot Americano. "Hailey Page? Underneath that sweet exterior is the heart of a viper," he says.

"How do you know that?" Felix asks.

"They used to go to summer camp together," I say. "Jude won't say anything more about it."

"Come on, fess up," Felix says.

Jude shakes his head. "No way. Lips sealed."

"The point is, she might know something," I say, "so we should talk to her."

The Arlington bell rings the ten-minute warning, and I feel myself pulled toward the sprawling brick building. For almost three years I heard that bell and hurried toward my homeroom. I can remember the weight of the backpack on my back and the squeak of tennis shoes on the polished concrete floors. I can almost feel the crush of people in the halls, the guys calling out to one another and slapping each other on the shoulder, the girls giddy to be reunited like they hadn't just seen each other yesterday afternoon.

It's like I'm on the other side of a high, invisible wall from them.

But not for long.

"All right, boys," I say, clapping my hands together. "Ready to go to school?"

28

"*This is completely and utterly insane,*" Jude says, and I know that he's right. But I push open the doors anyway.

And it's just like in the movies—the hall gets dead quiet, and everyone turns to look at us.

"Come on," I whisper. The three of us walk quickly through the path that's been cleared for us. Felix is softly cursing, probably because he can't believe he's following me. And Jude—wild, goofy Jude—he starts waving to everyone like he's still their beloved Fighting Tiger.

We just need to find Hailey before a teacher—or, worse, Palmieri—finds us. We pass the office without anyone stopping us, and then we hurry past the trophy case in the

main hall, where Parker's face smiles out from a photograph of last year's state champion football team.

"Hailey's homeroom is upstairs," Jude says. "I think
it's 211."

I wish her room were closer to an exit, but there's nothing I can do about it now. I check my watch. We have six
minutes until the bell rings.

When we get to the right room, Felix pokes his head in
and tells Hailey he needs to talk to her.

"Hey, F," she says, fluffing her hair as she comes out.
Then she sees us and her face twists in confusion. "What are
you guys doing here? Aren't you, like, expelled?" she asks.

"Yeah, but—" Jude begins.

"We have some questions for you," I say.

Felix adds, "And I'm just gonna film it—that cool?"

Hailey's lipsticked mouth immediately forms a sexy little pout as she turns toward him. She's one of those pretty
girls who love a camera and know it loves them back.

"It's about Parker Harris," I say.

"Oh, God," Hailey says, rolling her eyes. "Please don't
mention that name in my presence."

"I know you guys split up a few weeks ago," I say. "And
rumor has it he broke your heart."

Her bright smile falters. She gives her head a little shake.

"Hailey?"

Her expression is serious now. "I don't want to talk about it."

"Please," I say. "I'm just trying to figure some things out—like how that picture of him ended up on my Twitter, because it wasn't me who posted it. I thought maybe you could help."

Her eyes narrow. "So wait—you think *I* had something to do with it? Like I wanted to get him back or something?"

I shrug. "I don't know. Did you?"

"As if! I wasn't even at that party, or whatever you call it when idiots get shit-faced and take off their clothes in front of the football field."

"Someone could have texted you that picture," Jude points out. "And then maybe you got it posted. A revenge-served-cold sort of thing."

Hailey sniffs. "I wouldn't bother."

I decide to try a different tack. "Okay, maybe you didn't do it. But how'd you feel when the picture went public? Were you...I don't know, happy?"

"No, I wasn't *happy*. But Parker got what was coming to him," she says. "He's not who he pretends to be."

"What do you mean?" I ask.

"I mean you can't just hurt people like that," Hailey says heatedly.

Then Drew Portman comes out of the room and he slides his arm around Hailey's shoulders. "These dicks bugging you, babe?"

Hailey shakes her head. "I'm fine. They're just acting like the freaks they always were." She turns to Felix. "Except for you; you're all right. I saw your new video—the one where you fake-fall off your skateboard into traffic? That was totally brilliant. Let me know if you ever need an extra, because I'm available. I've been trying to build up a musical.ly following, and I don't know, we could, like, collaborate or something…"

Drew and Felix both look confused by this conversational turn. Felix sort of mumbles, "Yeah, sure," as Drew steers Hailey back into the classroom. I'm trying to figure out if I've learned anything or not when Jude elbows me and hisses, "Mosher at six o'clock."

And I don't even look up—I just start running, Jude tight on my heels.

Either Mr. Mosher's feeling particularly lazy this morning or luck seriously smiles on us for once, because we make it through the halls of Arlington without being caught. We stumble, laughing, into the gray morning, just as the piercing ring of the last tardy bell goes silent.

29

"Can I borrow Zelda?" I ask Jude once my heart's stopped pounding from our narrow escape.

"It's barely past 8 a.m.," he says, "and any sane man would go back to bed. But obviously you don't fall into that category. What do you need her for? Do you have an early tee time or something?"

"Yes, I've become an avid golfer in the last thirty-six hours," I joke. "My caddie says I'm still a bit of a duffer, though."

Jude narrows his eyes. "I can read you like a book. You want my car so you can go see Sasha."

He's right—but then again, it's not like it's that hard to guess. "I can drop you off?" I say hopefully.

Jude sighs and agrees, and twenty minutes later I'm pulling up in front of Sasha's house, just in time to see her come out her front door looking only half awake, her Matheson's apron tucked under her arm.

"What are you doing here?" she asks, squinting at me in the gray light. Her hair's pulled away from her face to reveal her tiny, perfect ears, with a pearl teardrop earring dangling from each tiny, perfect lobe. I've never seen Sasha's ears before, and as weird as it may sound, I have an almost overwhelming desire to kiss them.

That would probably get me killed—by her dad or by Sasha herself, take your pick.

"I came to apologize for being a dick yesterday." I reach down and pick up the roses, which are still on the corner of her porch. "I brought you these," I say.

She raises an eyebrow, because by now they're so totally wilted they look like used Kleenex on stems. "I mean, I brought them last night. They looked better then."

"Thanks," she says. "Should I put them in a vase?"

I shrug. "Or the compost pile, whatever. Anyway, I was hoping I could give you a ride to work," I say.

She looks over at Jude's car. "In that thing?"

"I thought you might be tired of riding around in your cute little vintage Saab. I thought you might like to experience the purple death trap known as Zelda, with your own personal chauffeur." I give a little half bow.

She smiles. "Well, if you put it that way." She climbs into the front seat and sees two coffees sitting in the cup-holders. "One for me?" she asks.

"For you," I say. "How long until you have to be at work?"

"Ninety minutes till I clock in," she says. "Sometimes I go in early to sit in Starbucks and read the *Times,* just to get out of the house."

"I want to take you to the Property—is that okay?"

She shrugs. "I've got coffee, I'm happy." Then she flashes a smile at me. "I mean, not *happy,* but you get the idea."

It seems to me like Sasha would, in the larger scheme of things, have a thousand reasons to be happy, but—*as we have established*—what the hell do I know? I'm no expert in anything, and least of all in Sasha Ellis.

I park near the dahlia patch and send up a flutter of sparrows. Curls of mist float above the surface of the pond like ghosts.

We sit on the edge of the deck, above the rustling cattails.

"I'm sorry I've been so focused on my own problems," I begin.

"Seriously," Sasha says, "don't worry about it. I was just having a bad day."

"Yeah, I've been having a few of those myself," I say.

She nods, gives a half laugh.

"I was so *hopeful* for a while," I say. "I mean, I thought we could really make something happen with the movie. But we've gone all around with our cameras and questions, and we still aren't any closer to the truth about who framed any of us." I take a sip of coffee. It's already cold. "My whole 'I want to write my own ending' isn't turning out the way I thought it would. And maybe it sounds like I'm giving myself a little pity party, but I sort of feel like it's time for me to catch a bit of a goddamn break."

"You must really miss your dad," she says suddenly.

It's a sentence that seems to take us both by surprise.

"Yeah," I say after breathing deeply for a minute. "I still can't believe that it happened, that it's true. It's like every single day I've got to learn it all over again—that I'm never going to see him again."

"I'm so sorry," she says softly.

You and me both, I think.

Because what, really, is there to say? I can't tell Sasha about my recurring dream of finding my dad still alive but bleeding to death before my eyes, the red running like a river down the backseat of our old car. Or what it feels like to wake in the middle of the night with a sadness so heavy I almost can't breathe. Or how my mom's been broken in half by her grief.

So for a little while we just sit there, watching the blue pond, its small ripples a sign of all that cold, fishy life below the surface.

"Can I ask you a question?" I eventually ask.

"Okay," she says.

"Where's your mom?"

Sasha gazes up toward the sky. "Chicago," she says. "I used to live with her there, you know. She was a painter."

"Like Jude," I say.

"But not at all like Jude. Because she stopped working on her art and started only caring about the art *scene*. It was cool at first, and kind of glamorous. But then she started partying a lot. It was like 'Oh, so-and-so's here from London with his gallerist, and I've got to show them we're not a bunch of corn-fed Illinois mouth breathers,' which apparently meant she had to go to really fancy restaurants and snort lines off the porcelain in the ladies' room."

"That's crazy," I say.

Sasha nods. "Things got pretty out of hand. She and my dad hadn't been together for a really long time, and back then I only saw him a couple of times a year. But then one summer she didn't come home for four nights in a row, and it started to seem like Pinewood might be a better place for me to be."

"So has it been better?" I ask hopefully.

Sasha reaches down, grabs the head of a cattail, and then tosses it into the water. "No," she says, "I wouldn't say so."

I guess I'm kind of surprised to hear this. "Do you honestly hate it here that much? Is it really so impossible to hang around with me in this beautiful place?" I ask, gesturing around us. "Does all this gorgeousness pain you or something?"

I'm trying to make a small and possibly unfunny joke out of it, because I feel like there's something wrong—something she's not telling me.

She says, quietly, "You guys are fine."

"Wow," I say, "thanks. That's awesome you feel so strongly about us."

She gives a short little bark of a laugh. "Sorry," she says. "You're better than fine."

"How much better?" I ask.

"Oh, stop," she says.

"Seriously, I want to know how many degrees past fine I am. Like five? Ten?"

She turns and smiles at me. She's so dazzling I can barely stand it.

"Do you know the poet Mary Oliver?" she asks.

I shake my head. I'm an uncultured hick compared to Sasha Ellis, and we both know it.

"Listen to this," she says.

"You do not have to be good.
You do not have to walk on your knees
for a hundred miles through the desert, repenting.
You only have to let the soft animal of your body
    love what it loves.
Tell me about despair, yours, and I will tell you mine.
Meanwhile the world goes on.
Meanwhile the sun and the clear pebbles of the rain
are moving across the landscapes,
over the prairies and the deep trees,
the mountains and the rivers.
Meanwhile the wild geese, high in the clean blue air,
are heading home again.
Whoever you are, no matter how lonely,
the world offers itself to your imagination,
calls to you like the wild geese, harsh and exciting—
over and over announcing your place
in the family of things."

Sasha's voice cracks when she says the word *family,* and
she cuts off abruptly.

"Wow," I say, "that's really good."

There's a pause, and to lighten the mood, I ask, "So you
memorized the whole thing, huh? That's not impressive."

I smirk at her, but Sasha won't look me in the eye.

I put my hand over her hand. "Are you okay? Wait—
I know you're not okay. You hate that word. But if you
didn't hate that word, could you apply it to yourself?"

She smiles. "That's a funny question."

"I mean it, though. Are you all right?"

"I don't know," she says.

Her voice sounds so small. And when I look over at her,
I see a single tear running down her pale cheek.

"Hey," I say, "what's wrong?"

Fiercely, she wipes it away. "Don't ask. I can't talk about it."

Uncertain of what else to do, I fold my fingers around
hers. She doesn't say anything, but she lets me keep them
there.

30

"Do *you think there's something weird* going on with Sasha?" I ask Jude's back.

We're in his garage again—which is now his full-time studio since it's too full of canvases and stretcher bars to accommodate a car. I'm perched on a stool, and he's standing in front of a large rectangular canvas that's half covered in swirling color.

"Sasha Ellis, as a conversation topic, is getting a little stale," Jude says, adding a blue flourish to an abstract shape. "No offense."

"I just feel like there's something she's not telling me."

"She's a complicated girl, and there're probably a *million* things she's not telling you. But do you want to know my hypothesis?"

"Sure."

"She's still got feelings for Parker."

I feel like I've been sucker punched. "What are you talking about?"

"She's against him on an aesthetic and political level, because he's such an unparalleled bro. On the other hand, he's hot, and he's a Superman type, which is hard to resist."

"First of all, just because he's a handsome jock doesn't make him a hero. And second of all, what does she need a Superman type for?"

"Have you ever *seen* a Hollywood movie? All girls want to be rescued."

"That's completely and totally sexist."

Jude shrugs. "Hey, I wouldn't mind being rescued by a big handsome hulk, either."

"Rescued from *what?*" I ask.

"I don't know, *everything.* Can you sit still? I'm trying to paint you into this picture."

"Is that weird bug-eyed thing supposed to be me?"

"Don't you see the likeness?"

"Not really," I say.

Jude squints, points his paintbrush at it. "Yeah, you're right. You're not nearly as handsome."

"You're hilarious," I say. "And you're wrong about Sasha."

He shrugs again. "Only time will tell." He dips a brush

into a smear of bright azure oil paint. "God, I love Phthalo Blue," he sighs as he turns his attention to the canvas again.

And the thing is, Jude really *is* good at what he does. He's probably going to get a scholarship to RISD, and pretty soon he'll be represented by a fancy Chelsea gallery, and the next thing you know, I'll see a picture of him in *Artforum,* drinking champagne next to Jackson Pollock.

Well, not actually Jackson Pollock, because he's been dead for sixty years, but you get the idea.

Meanwhile, what do I have to offer the world? A few decent articles in the school newspaper and a documentary film that is so far a complete and utter failure? I've conducted interviews of three POIs, I've got tons of footage to go over, and I'm no closer to figuring out who posted the infamous picture.

Things just aren't looking that good for me.

I grab Jude's phone, turn on the video, and flip the camera setting so I'm staring right into the lens for a video selfie. "What am I going to do?" I ask it—as if it could possibly have an answer.

Jude doesn't turn around. "What do you mean?"

I set the phone down and prop it against some art stuff so we're both in the shot. If I can't film any answers, I guess I can at least film my struggle. "If I can't prove we're all innocent," I say. "If I can't make this whole nightmare go away."

"News flash: we're not all innocent," Jude says.

"Right, I know. Parker's guilty of being a stupid drunken idiot. So really—maybe he's not such a superhero after all."

"Maybe Sasha's attracted to his dark side."

"Please. Even Parker's dark side is boring jock stuff. *He secretly can't really bench 210. Oh, no!*"

"God, dude, you are relentless. You know what? I'll bet you a million dollars that Sasha took the soda money."

Sucker punched *again*. "What are you talking about?"

"Troubled little rich girl," he says. "It's so cliché."

"Sasha isn't a cliché!"

"Your love for her is getting *embarrassing*. Look, she's brilliant, possibly insane, and she works a shitty job when she doesn't need the money—which, okay, is mildly interesting. She's gorgeous, she has buckets of charisma she couldn't hide if she tried, and she makes all the boys fall in love with her. That sounds like Manic Pixie Dreamgirl territory, my friend—which, news flash again, is a *cliché*."

"None of this has anything to do with the soda money. What makes you think she took it?"

"I'm an artist. I see into people's souls."

"You are so full of shit!"

"She's guilty."

"How can you say that about her? Where's your evidence? You hear her jangling when she walks?"

"She's not dumb enough to go around with pockets full of quarters, Theo. *God.*"

"I can't believe you'd just accuse her like that. You're worse than Palmieri. You have no hard evidence—just one of your *feelings*. You're sick of the uncertainty, so you just want to have a solution to the problem and a neat little end to the story." I'm stomping around the garage by now—screw staying in the shot—but Jude's still painting like nothing's going on at all. "Meanwhile, look at you! You act all innocent, but it's your damn mascot head in the photo! Maybe *you're* the guilty one."

Jude jabs his paintbrush into the canvas. "Yeah, and maybe *you* posted the photo—on *your* stupid Twitter account!"

"You've got to be kidding me," I say.

"*You've* got to be kidding *me*."

"Why are you being such a dick?"

"Why are you being such a whiny little shit?"

I clench my fists. "Do you want to turn around and look at me when you say that?"

Jude takes his brush, dips it in black, and just like that, the face that was supposed to be me is an ugly dark blob.

"Go home," he says. "I'm working."

And since it's either that or get in fisticuffs with my best friend, I do what he tells me.

31

After the fight with Jude, I only want to be alone, but when I get home I find my mom sitting on the porch with a glass of iced tea and a bag of Cheetos.

"What are you doing here?" I blurt.

"I live here," she says, smiling.

Barely is the word I quickly stop myself from saying.

She squints up at me. "Is something wrong?" she asks.

"No," I lie. I try to slide past her, but she pats the other Adirondack chair.

"Sit. Have a talk with your old mom."

I know that's my cue to say *You're not old,* but I keep my mouth shut. I can't cheer her up today. I just don't have it in me.

"I took the rest of the day off," she says. "I thought I'd cook, and then we could have a nice dinner together."

"You left work before noon just so you could make dinner?"

She smiles. "I'm rusty in the kitchen."

No shit, I think. My body is basically 98 percent frozen burrito.

"I guess it's kind of silly, but seriously, hon, who knows how long spaghetti and meatballs might take me?" She gives a little laugh. "What do you think? Does that sound good?"

"Sure." Though after what just happened with Jude, I'm finding it hard to feel enthused.

My mom sighs and runs her hands through her hair. "Okay, Theo, full disclosure."

I promptly sit down. *Full disclosure?* What are the chances of me liking whatever's coming next? "Go on," I say.

"I told myself that I was going to clean out your father's things today. That's why I came home early. And I started. But, God, it was so hard." She shakes her head. "I picked up the sweater I bought him the Christmas before last. That nice green wool one—do you remember it? I don't know if he ever even wore it. It was such a beautiful sweater. And I was holding it and then I just started *screaming,* Theo. I screamed like a crazy woman. *'How could you do this? How could you leave us?*'" She wipes tears away from her eyes. "It's a miracle the neighbors didn't call the cops on me."

I suck in my breath. Most of the time I try not to think about my dad—I try not to let the pain in. But it's always there, no matter what. It's just waiting for me to pay attention to it. "I've asked myself the same questions," I say quietly.

She hands me the Cheetos bag and I reach in. There's nothing but crumbs.

"Do you think you could help me?" she asks.

I brush my orange fingertips against my jeans. "How?"

"We could go through his clothes together," she says, her voice a quiet plea. "We'll find a place to donate most of them. But maybe you want some things. Like his USC sweatshirt and his good suit."

But grief makes me bitter. "What does a kid with no future need a suit for?" I scowl. "My first court date? A date with a probation officer?"

My mom's eyes are green and sad. "Don't be so hard on yourself."

"Why not? Everyone else is," I say.

"Oh, Theo," she sighs.

For a second I think she's going to say something else, but she just shakes her head. And I know she's in pain, but

I can't help but wish she'd make some tiny stab at cheering me up for once, some small attempt to take care of me.

"Well," I say after another minute. "I'm going to make myself some lunch. I can feel my blood burrito level dipping."

I stand up and start to go inside when she says, "Wait." She takes a deep breath. "I also got some news today—interesting news. Maybe even good."

"What?"

"Someone wants to buy the Property."

My heart seizes up in my chest, and I feel like I'm going to be sick. This is exactly what I've been afraid of. I try to speak but I can't. My mouth just opens and closes uselessly.

"Theo?" my mom asks. "Are you okay?"

This *utterly* ridiculous question is what gets my vocal cords working—*loudly*. "What do you mean?" I yell. "Did you put it up for sale without telling me?"

"No, I would never do that! But, Theo, I can't just keep paying for it. I can barely handle the mortgage on our house."

"But you can't sell it!" I cry. "You just *can't!* It would be the worst thing you could do."

Her fingers tighten their grip on the chair. "Says who? Do you think I should work day and night so you can have a place to party with your friends—is that it?"

I can feel the tears, but I won't let them come. "It's not *about* me. It was your place—yours and Dad's!"

"But then he left me, Theo. He left *us*. That beautiful dream we had? It died with him. Whether we keep the Property or not, there's no changing that."

"You can't sell it," I say. I'm not yelling anymore. I'm barely even whispering.

"I'm not saying I want to, baby. I'm saying I might have to."

If the Property gets sold, what do I have left?

It feels a lot like nothing.

"I thought you'd be...not happy, maybe, but relieved," my mom says.

"Dad and I built that deck," I say. "We dug all those raised beds. We fished there. We hung all those stupid novelty lights! That's all I have left of him."

I'm wiping tears from my face and my mom is looking wrecked.

"Oh, Theo," she says. "It's not all you have left."

"Please don't tell me how I have his eyes or his smile or some shit like that," I say.

She shakes her head. "No, I don't mean that. Earlier, when I started going through his things, I found this in the safe." She holds out an envelope. It's sealed, and on the front, there's my dad's handwriting.

For Theo, it says.

32

And I'd thought the day couldn't get more awful.

I go upstairs to my room and put the letter on the desk where I used to do my homework, between my copies of *The Great Gatsby* and *Catch-22*. I can tell by his handwriting, which is shaky, that my dad wrote it after he got sick.

What did he need to say to me that he couldn't say to my face? That he was scared? That he was sorry for what he was about to do? That he was bitter and enraged he'd received a death sentence at age forty-three?

What if he wrote about how he needed me to be good and to take care of Mom? Because obviously I've done a terrible job of that. Can the dead be disappointed in the living?

I don't want to know the answer to that question.

Maybe not opening the letter makes me seem like a coward. And maybe I really *am* one. But I'm also standing on the thin edge of a pretty goddamn deep existential abyss, and I really don't want to fall in.

I've lost my father, my school, and my reputation. I'm also on the verge of losing my best friend.

In other words: shit must change. And for the better this time.

I've got to make something good happen—something good to balance out all the bad. So what do I do?

I need to apologize to Jude, first of all, and I've got to give Sasha something to feel happy about. And maybe we need to celebrate at the Property, before that gets taken away, too.

Then, amid all the suckage of my current life, I get a brilliant idea.

This means that I have to go to Matheson's again; it's ridiculous but necessary that I see Sasha face-to-face.

Sure enough, she rolls her eyes when she sees me walk in the door. "Seriously, creeper, are you trying to destroy my career in customer service?" she asks.

"I saw your manager outside on a smoke break," I say, "and anyway, if you did get fired for some reason, I happen to know that the 7-Eleven is hiring."

"Oh, great, thanks," Sasha says. "I've always wanted to sell Big Gulps to pizza-faced twelve-year-olds and Labatts to creepy dudes in wifebeaters."

"Sounds like fun, doesn't it? I have to warn you, though, it's a very competitive application process."

"Okay, so don't get me fired here, all right?"

I grab a pair of reading glasses from the display right near her register and put them on. "Now I'm in disguise," I say, squinting at a suddenly huge, blurry Sasha-shaped blob. "I am a brand-new customer of your fine establishment. Do you give discounts to the visually challenged?"

"You're acting super weird," she says. "What's up?"

"I actually have a really important question to ask you," I say.

"Then go ahead and ask it," she says.

"Will you go to the prom with me?"

She just stares at me.

"Well?" I say.

"You're an idiot," she says. "We're expelled. We aren't allowed to go to A Night in Paris, or whatever our stupid prom theme is this year."

"Not the school prom," I say, unable to suppress a grin. "The Convict Prom."

"And what fresh hell is *that?*" Sasha asks.

"We're going to have a prom at the Property," I say. "All

of us who were expelled, plus anyone else who isn't too chickenshit to hang out with us. I'm talking music, lights, awkward, uncoordinated dancing—the whole shebang."

"You're insane," she says.

"That is *not* the first time someone has said that to me lately," I say. "So what do you think—are you in?"

And it seems like Sasha smiles for real now, though it's hard to see through the Coke-bottle glasses. "Yeah, okay," she says. "I'll be there."

"Remember to dress up," I say. I remove the readers and the world snaps back into focus, just in time for me to catch her rolling her eyes at me again.

"Duh," she says. "But if you wear a rental tux, I'm absolutely not dancing with you."

"Don't worry," I say. "No rented polyester. Now I have to go apologize to Jude and do a little party planning."

"Streamers are on sale, you know," she says. "Aisle 6."

"Awesome. You be in charge of streamers. I'll take care of everything else."

33

On the night of the Convict Prom, every single chili pepper and cactus light in the gazebo is blazing in Technicolor. I found all of our old Christmas lights, too, and I wrapped a dozen strands of them around the railings of the deck. Their reflections in the water make the still surface look like it's dotted with jewels.

Jude's contribution to the decorations was *every single rose* from each of his mom's prized rose bushes, which he cut and arranged in canning jars. (She's not going to be happy about that.) And he's wearing an actual tuxedo— a vintage Christian Dior, he claims, which he found at a church rummage sale for fifteen bucks.

"If only I had my tiger head, my outfit would be complete," Jude says wistfully.

I decided to wear my dad's suit, even though it's big on me. My shirt's open at the neck and I have no tie; I'm not even wearing dress shoes, just my Chucks.

It's my dance, though, so I figure I can wear whatever the hell I want.

Felix and his camera are at the edge of the deck, waiting to film people as they arrive: a delinquent's processional at a Convict Prom, aka the footage I plan to use during my documentary's end credits.

If the people arrive, that is. I have no idea who, if anyone, is going to show up. I put Jude in charge of the invites because he promised he'd be able to work some of his old mascot charm. Maybe we're still the town pariahs, and maybe we're not. Only tonight will tell.

Parker, whom I wouldn't have invited if I had a choice, shows up with a keg, and suddenly I like him a notch better than I had before. I brought the wine still left over from my dad's wake, and we've set up a table with a bunch of potato chips, Doritos, and pretzels.

It's 8 p.m., and the sky's turning to lavender. We've got a jerry-rigged but decent sound system, festive lights, and alcohol.

But so far we've got no actual guests.

"Remember," Jude says, patting my shoulder reassuringly, "people like to be fashionably late."

But he, too, looks a little nervous about attendance. He crams a fistful of Cool Ranch Doritos into his mouth and says, as crumbs fall out, "But, man, we've got a *lot* of shit to consume if it's just us here tonight."

Parker says, "I'm going to get to work on that keg. You pussies want to join me?"

"Maybe later, bro," I say, and he actually tries to give me a high five, but I dodge it.

Half an hour later, after I've had a beer and about a pound of potato chips, I'm thrilled to see the approaching headlights of a car.

"Okay, you guys, here we go," Jude says excitedly. "Our first glamorous guests! Felix, roll camera!"

But Jude was wrong about the glamour, and the *s* on the end of guest, too. It's only Jere7my, who's wearing a Star Wars T-shirt and a clip-on tie that seems to have math equations printed on it. He heaves a case of Tecate onto the chips table and scowls. "There's more where this came from if no one throws me into the lake," he says grouchily.

And then the five of us stand around dumbly while the sky deepens to violet and bats go swooping and cartwheeling through the air above us. The Property looks more beautiful than it ever has. But I'm probably not the only one who's wondering if this seemingly brilliant idea was actually a huge mistake.

Jude, trying to boost morale, puts on Prince and starts dancing all by himself, which Felix, for lack of anything better to do, films.

"I don't know what place your goofy dancing will have in our documentary," I call.

"Only the truly innocent could move this freely," Jude retorts, waving his arms over his head. "It's just more evidence in my favor."

"We've got to have a lot of footage," Felix reminds me. "This is what we call an establishing shot. And who knows what you'll want in post-production. You can't be shy with clip length."

Considering that I'm the one who's supposedly directing this movie, is it bad that I have no idea what he's talking about? I take a slug of beer and throw a handful of chips in my mouth. "Okay, yeah, sure, keep rolling," I mumble.

"Great party," Jere7my says drily.

"You probably don't have much to compare it to," I snap.

"Point taken," he says. "Cheers."

"Did you think any more about who might have gotten into my computer?" I ask. "Anything else you'd like to say on record? I've got a clip mic."

Jere7my shakes his head. "Nope."

"Great. Thanks so much for your help."

"I have my own problems, as you might possibly be able to imagine," Jere7my says.

"Your mom won't let you buy a sixty-four-inch screen for your World of Warcraft games?"

Jere7my gives a little sneery smile. "Very funny."

"Come on, it was mildly amusing."

"*Mildly* being the operative word," Jere7my allows.

"What are you two nut sacks talking about?" Parker asks, lumbering over. He tips up a Solo cup and downs twelve ounces of Bud in about three seconds.

"Jere-seven-my was hoping you'd ask him to dance," I say.

Jere7my pales. "No offense, I'm sure you're a great dancer, but that's the last thing I'd ever—"

"Come on, dude," Parker barks. And I'm stunned to see him grab Jere7my and spin him around. Because he's *smiling*. Like this is actually *fun*.

"I'm going to…regurgitate," Jere7my manages to say.

Parker gives him another few good whirls and then stops. "You just need beer, little dude." And then he hands him one.

Jude shimmies over next to me. "It's *amazetits* to see the jock talking to the nerd. Amazetits…is that better than amazeballs? It isn't, is it? I need to find a new word entirely. Anyway! The Convict Prom is bringing people together."

"Just not any *girl* people yet," I say.

Jude says, "Well, I did bring a dress just in case."

"Maybe you should think about putting it on."

But right then I see Sasha's Saab coming down the gravel road, and my heart gives a little leap of happiness and relief.

"Saved by the eternally unpredictable Sasha Ellis," Jude says, smoothing his silk lapels. "Thank goodness, because I don't like the heels I brought."

When Sasha steps out of the car, she is... well, I guess the word might be *resplendent*. She's wearing a clinging pale golden gown, and her hair's pulled up into a high loose knot, with tiny curling tendrils falling into her face. I swear she's almost glowing.

She is also—beautifully, absurdly—draped in *yards* of crepe paper streamers.

"Pick your chin up off the deck. You're making a spectacle of yourself," Jere7my says. "Then again, so is she."

I run toward Sasha and she holds out her arms. "I'm here, I'm here!" she says.

"You are," I say, laughing, so glad to see her I could almost cry. "And I see you really went for it with the sale streamers."

"They were such a bargain, I couldn't resist." She unwraps a blue streamer from her shoulders and puts it around mine. "There," she says. "Much better."

And it almost doesn't matter who else comes and what happens next; this is all I need.

34

It's as if Sasha has some kind of magnetic power, because right after she arrives, a dozen more people show up, including Jenna Tucker and Lulu Trinh, trailed by their dates, the twins Aiden and Caden Dorsey, who've always been indistinguishable to me. (One's wearing a blue bow tie and the other, black—but who is who? It's impossible to say.)

Jude plays the gracious host, flitting from person to person and offering them drinks and snacks. Felix switches the music to something with a deeper, funkier beat while Sasha perches near him on the railing, filming everyone with one of his little cameras. Jenna and her Dorsey start dancing, and pretty soon they're trying to get other people to come join them.

I have to say, it feels like a real party. But is that what I wanted—just another party? Or do I want a night that gives me answers? A night that tells me what went wrong and where I stand and what the future might hold for me?

A few of Parker's football bros roll up in a Hummer ("Alert, alert, douchemobile incoming," Jere7my mutters), accompanied by a trio of girls from the tennis team in matching strapless dresses. A station wagon ejects a handful of freshmen, who look around with big, wide eyes as if they can't believe they've managed to ascend to these dizzying social heights.

Jude makes one of his mother's roses into a boutonniere for Chip Hoffman's lapel, and Chip—a starting linebacker—gives him a high five so enthusiastic it nearly knocks Jude over. And while I wouldn't say that I'm being greeted like a long-lost friend or anything, at least no one's looking at me like delinquency is a disease they can catch.

"Who's the host with the most?" Jude says, watching Chip join a mini dance circle near the keg. "That's a rhetorical question. It's *you*, Theo Foster! Look at all these people! They're having a blast! Long live the Convict Prom!"

I tap my Solo cup against his. I know I'm supposed to relax and enjoy myself, but I really just want to ask them all about the Picture: who they think took it and who was behind our expulsion. Would they believe us now if we said we were innocent? Or do they just no longer care who did what?

I crook my finger at Sasha, summoning her and the camera. She slides off the railing and takes small, awkward steps toward me. She wobbles, reaches out, and grabs my shoulder. "What was I thinking, wearing stilettos?" she mutters. "They're nothing but an oppressive symbol of traditional heteronormative femininity."

"What?"

"These shoes suck," she says. She bends down, slips off the pair of gold high heels, and then sighs in relief. "There. Much better."

She seems suddenly tiny, and I resist the urge to put my arm around her shoulder protectively. Sasha Ellis doesn't need my protection.

"I want you to help me film Chip," I say.

"Doing his white boy dab?" she asks skeptically. "That could be some good blackmail material, I guess." She grins at me. "Or maybe we're making a dance movie now? Against my better judgment, I did love *Step Up 2: The Streets.*"

"I haven't seen it, but no need to explain your references to me," I say. "Anyway, dope, I want to interview him. I want to ask him about the infamous Parker party," I say.

She pokes me in the chest. "I admire your dedication to

this film project. But call me dope again on pain of death, Foster."

I hold up my hands—*I surrender!*—and together we walk over to Chip. He turns toward us, his eyes already cloudy with beer or maybe a few too many concussions on the football field.

"Hey, Chip," I say. "Good to see you, uh, bro. How's it going?"

Chip grunts a word that sounds like "good."

"Awesome. Great. I hope you like those jalapeño Cheetos—pretty spicy, huh? But I gotta ask you something. How does this party compare to the one in the Arlington end zone?" I ask.

"Huh?" he says.

"You know—the party that got Parker expelled. Remember the story that was all over Channel 6? About the picture with the whiskey and the breasts? You were there that night, weren't you?"

He nods. "Yeah, dude, that was a rager."

"Yeah, it looked like it. Hey, do you happen to know who was wearing the tiger head that night?" I ask casually.

"Besides Tigger? Who knows?" He shakes his big bear-like head. "I was tore up that night, bro. I did six Jäger shots and woke up under the bleachers."

"That's unfortunate," Sasha mutters from behind the camera.

Chip shrugs. "Wasn't the first time."

"What do you mean 'besides Tigger'?" I demand.

"I mean your boy Jude got the tiger head out."

"*Jude* was with you?" I say.

"Okay, you're kinda dense for a nerd. Like I said, Tigger was there. Tigger got the tiger head. Tigger put it on his own head."

But this *can't* mean... "Did someone wear it after he did? Did he, like, loan it to anyone?" I ask.

Chip rolls his eyes. "I have no idea. I told you—the Jäger knocked me out cold."

Sasha brings the camera down. "In that case, Mr. Hoffman, thank you for your assistance. Please continue your pathetic attempts at dancing." She dismisses him with a wave of her hand and then turns to me. "I guess we better go talk to *your boy*," she says.

35

My head's spinning, and it's not from the beer. I push my way through the crowd until I find Jude leaning against the side of the gazebo. His tux jacket is still on, but he's taken off his shirt. With his hairless chest, black bow tie, and carefully styled hair, he looks like an underfed Chippendale dancer.

Sasha trains the camera on the two of us, and Felix wanders over to see what's up.

"You were *at that party*," I accuse him.

Jude blinks slowly at me. He knows exactly what I'm talking about. "And?" he says, a hint of challenge in his voice.

"So why didn't you ever admit that to me? Why'd you

let me think that someone stole the tiger head from the locker room?"

"This is good," Felix says. "When the pack turns on itself."

"Shut up," Sasha hisses.

"You were wearing the tiger head that night!" I accuse him. "Why'd you *lie?*"

Jude stands up straighter. "Yeah, fine, I was," he says. "I was there. The baseball team had just crushed Lincoln, fourteen to two, and I was suffering from an excess of school spirit, okay? The whole thing was totally spontaneous."

"So you were drunk in your tiger head."

"Guilty," Jude says. "So what."

"I can't believe you didn't tell me! What else do I not know? *Was it you who pissed—*"

Jude cuts me off with a slice of his hand. "First of all, Sherlock, there isn't enough alcohol in the world to get me to whip out my junk in front of the jock brigade. And second of all, do you even remember the Picture? The pisser is wearing *cargo shorts.* I wouldn't be caught dead in cargo shorts. Even if I *did die* and someone dressed my corpse in cargo shorts, I would *come back from the afterlife to make a costume change!* And I can't even believe that you'd *ever* consider the possibility that—"

I interrupt him because I realize I don't need him to say

anything more. This is a repeat of our fight in his garage and I just got him to forgive me. "I'm sorry," I say. "I know. You're right. It could never have been you. But—dude, why didn't you tell me you partied with Parker Harris?"

"I have my arty reputation to keep up." Jude doesn't look at me when he says this.

"Are you guys, like, friends?"

"No, we're not friends. Isn't that obvious? We've merely been at social gatherings simultaneously. Like this one."

"I don't think anything's obvious anymore," I say. "And I don't know why you had to keep anything a secret from me." I can't tell him that I'm hurt or even really explain why I am.

I look over at Parker. He's by the snack table, laughing at Chip's relentlessly terrible dancing. He looks happy— maybe happier than I've ever seen him. Like he just won the state championship football game *and* a lottery scratch-off. And once again I think about how unfair it is that the only one of us who's actually guilty is also the only one who hasn't actually suffered.

I motion Sasha and the camera to follow me as I walk right up to him and stop; my head comes almost to his shoulders. "You'd better hope no one posts a picture of *this* party, huh?"

It takes a minute for Parker to process what I'm talking

about. Then he looks down at the beer bottle he's holding and goes, "Yeah, I guess."

"Of course, we're filming everything," I add. "So maybe something'll find its way onto YouTube."

He's totally unfazed. "School year's almost done, bro. Chase'll keep me until then."

This pisses me off. "You don't care, do you? You're untouchable. And what's so crazy is that you don't even give a shit that *I'm* supposedly the one who posted the picture."

"But you said you didn't," Parker says.

"And you just *believe* me."

"Why not?" he asks.

"You don't know me! Maybe I'm a pathological liar. I don't get it—if the whole world thinks that I got you expelled, how come *you* don't?"

Parker says, "I don't care who got me expelled. It's worked out great for me."

What I'd give to be big enough to throw a punch at his perfect cheekbones. "You're digging that preppy asshole factory your dad sent you to, huh? You like those cravats?"

"Still don't know what a cravat is," Parker says, shrugging. "But listen, man, you got to loosen up. This is a party! It's almost summer. Chill out! Have a fucking brew, yo. Let's just be cool." And then, unbelievably, he holds out his hand for me to shake. "Come on. Buds?"

I stare at it—the big pink paw that threw a record-breaking number of touchdowns last football season. That clutched the Jack Daniels in the infamous Picture. That once held Sasha's slender fingers as they walked together down the halls.

"Shake his hand," Sasha whispers.

I don't want to do it, but I don't want to cause a scene, either. I'm the host, aren't I? I should try to be gracious. And so I reach out, and my palm meets Parker's. When he grips my hand in his, my bones feel like matchsticks he could crush. But he doesn't crush them. He gives me a big, friendly grin and then slaps me on the back with his other giant paw. "Thanks, bro," he says. "Killer party."

36

I know I'm supposed to let it go. But I just can't. There are twenty people from my high school here—which means twenty potential interview subjects. There's got to be *someone* here with a clue.

I go find the twins and ask them to follow me into the gazebo, where Felix has positioned one of his cameras on a tripod. They look around in mild but good-natured confusion as Sasha tugs on their arms, forcing them to sit down on one of the old couches.

"This here is kind of like our confession cam," I say. "You know, like on *Real World* or whatever."

The twins blink at me. It's truly *eerie* how alike they look.

"Say your names for the camera, please," Sasha commands them, and they do as they're told.

"Okay," Aiden (blue bow tie) then says. "So now what? We're supposed to tell you our deep dark secrets or something?"

"Do you have any?" I ask.

"Not really," says Caden (black bow tie).

"They're simple men," Sasha says. "Or is it *man,* singular, since they're genetically identical?"

"Actually, due to copy error mutations, identical twins tend to have many genetic differences," Jere7my points out. "Human DNA contains approximately six gigabytes of information, and—"

"I'm hoping you guys can help me," I interrupt before Jere7my goes down some coding rabbit hole. "I'm still trying to figure out how that picture of Parker got onto my Twitter. Have you heard any rumors about it?"

"I heard the topless girl's a sophomore at Lincoln," Aiden volunteers.

"That's interesting," I say, though honestly I don't care who she is, unless she posted the picture because she decided the world ought to see her breasts—which is *highly* improbable. "Have you heard anything else?"

The Dorseys shake their heads. "Sorry, man," Caden mumbles.

"Do you think I posted it?"

"I don't know," Caden says, and at the same moment Aiden goes, "I don't really care."

I sigh. These two are useless, and I immediately vow to forget which one is which.

"Dismissed," Sasha says, barely hiding her disgust as the twins head for the keg.

Jere7my cracks open a Tecate and says, "I'm not implying the human genome is actually *code*—that executes its genes to build us or anything. It's more like it gives us component blueprints—"

"Anyway," I interrupt. "Moving on."

A couple of freshmen stumble in, and Sasha waves them over. "Sit," she says. "Tell us what you know about the infamous picture of Parker."

A skinny kid with dark hair starts to grin. "Theo, right?" he says to me. "You fucked up Parker's shit big time. Nice work."

"Yeah, that was awesome," his friend says. Then he shoots me a puzzled look. "I don't get why Parker's here, though. Did he just forgive you?"

Sasha says, "Theo didn't post the picture, you barely sentient protohumans. That's why he's asking people about it. Also, I don't know why *you're* here, considering none of us has any idea who you are. Did your mommies say you could be out past ten?"

The first kid looks at me. "Really? It wasn't you?" He's obviously disappointed.

I sigh. "Cut," I say.

But Felix shakes his head. "We just keep the camera running," he says. "You need an hour of shooting to make five minutes in a final cut. A lot of documentaries have a shooting ratio of, like, sixty to one—"

I don't bother to listen to the rest of what he's saying. I push through the screen door and stomp out onto the deck.

"Don't *any* of you know what happened the night we beat Lincoln?" I yell over the thumping bass. "Doesn't one *single solitary person* know who took that fucking picture that got me expelled?"

Everyone turns to stare at me.

"Chill out, Theo," Lulu Trinh says. "You're throwing a party, not an inquisition."

"Yeah, have a brew and relax," Parker calls. He moves through the crowd and says, "Let me show you how it's done." Then he slides over to Sasha's side. "Want to dance?"

Sasha flashes her eyes at me. I don't want Parker anywhere near her, but I'm not her boyfriend or her protector.

I'm just the guy with the party real estate and the questions that no one seems to be able to answer.

I can't read Sasha's expression as she lets Parker whirl her away.

Someone hands me a bottle of something, and I take a big gulp. It's like swallowing fire. I cough and wipe my eyes. I take another swig.

On the far end of the deck, Parker's trying to coax Sasha into moonwalking with him. Jenna and one of the twins are making out by the snack table while Chip Hoffman and the other twin are daring each other to jump into the pond fully clothed. Jere7my reaches out, grabs a strand of chili pepper lights, and wraps it around his body.

"The yeti's moving in on your dame," Jere7my says. "And no one cares about your movie."

"She's not my dame," I say bitterly. "And take those lights off. You look like an anemic Christmas tree."

"You look like a lovesick douche canoe," Jere7my retorts. He hands me the bottle of whatever it is. "Cheers."

I grab it by the neck and vow not to let it go.

37

I awake on a gazebo couch in the pink dawn, a ratty afghan tucked around me.

Someone's snoring on the other couch, and someone else—Jude maybe?—is asleep on a lawn chair outside. Out on the deck are a few human-shaped lumps, cozily wrapped in sleeping bags they must have pulled from our old shed.

I step outside, rubbing my eyes. The deck is littered with Solo cups and chip crumbs. The pond is still and peaceful, but the birds are making a wild, chattering racket. The dawn chorus, my dad used to call it. We listened to it every morning we fished the pond, and hearing it now hurts.

"Good morning, sunshine," someone mumbles.

I turn and see Jere7my coming out of the bushes. There

are leaves in his hair, and a tattered blanket clings to his shoulders. "My mom is going to kill me," he says.

"If you hurry, maybe you can get home before she wakes up," I offer.

"That'd be no problem at all, assuming I could *fly*." He brushes a twig from his sweater. "I lost my car keys."

"Sorry to hear that," I say.

"Not as sorry as I am," he says grimly. "If I'm forced to engage in any more rituals of adolescent socialization and/or interpersonal connection, I'm going to break out in hives." He crouches down and starts feeling around under the chairs for his keys.

"Do you want help?"

He shakes his head. "No, thank you. I prefer to suffer my humiliations alone, as usual."

So I leave him to his search while I start gathering up the trash. I wave to two bleary-eyed sophomores perched in the grounded rowboat, who clearly didn't even try to go to sleep last night.

There are still half a dozen cars parked in the field. A few of them seem to have people asleep inside. Parker's pickup is still here, too, and as I walk closer to it, I see that the back gate is down, and there are sleeping bodies in the truck bed. Sticking out from underneath the blankets are two pairs of bare feet: one big and one tiny.

And lying in the grass nearby, tossed aside like an empty Solo cup, is a single gold high-heeled shoe.

I can feel last night's alcohol dulling my thoughts. My heart, too, thuds dully. I'm exhausted and raw.

Sasha was wearing gold stilettos—those *oppressive symbols of traditional heteronormative femininity*—last night.

I hear Jude calling my name in an awkward whisper-yell. I ignore him. I walk to the side of the truck and peer into the bed. I see dark, tousled hair, a pale arm thrown across the broad golden chest of Parker Harris.

She was never yours, Theo, I think.

But that doesn't make it hurt any less. I realize I'm holding my breath. The air wavers in front of my eyes and the still pond seems to dance with sudden ripples.

"Sasha," I whisper. "Sasha."

She doesn't move.

I stare at the thin, smooth shoulder, the long, white arm. Ever so gently, I reach out and touch her.

She murmurs in her sleep and turns over.

And it's not Sasha.

It's Parker's ex, Hailey Page.

My knees go weak, and I hold on to the truck so they don't buckle. I've never been so relieved in my life.

Jude's walking toward me now. "Do you think Gold

Star would deliver doughnuts if I begged? We could take up a collection." He's wearing just his tux pants and his bow tie now, and his hair's sticking up like he's been electrocuted by a malfunctioning set of novelty lights. He stops when he sees my face. "You thought that was Sasha in there, didn't you? But it's that viper instead."

"Where is she? Did you see her leave?"

"I don't know where she is, Theo! I don't watch her constantly, okay? I'm not her babysitter or her parole officer or whatever that hot mess needs."

"I just want to make sure she's okay."

"Do we really need to go over this again? Sasha Ellis can take care of herself. She always has. Now come here and give your best friend a hug, because we threw an awesome party. It's going to be *legendary*." He grabs me, squeezes me around the waist, and says, "Okay, that's better. Now where the hell is the coffee?"

In the gazebo I find a hotpot, a tin of very old Folgers, and a handful of chipped mugs. I proceed to make what my dad used to call cowboy coffee, which is where the grounds just float around in the hot water and you have to strain them through your teeth. It's terrible, obviously, but Jude and I both need the caffeine so badly we don't care.

When our guests wake up, bedheaded and bloodshot, we offer them a swig of it and send them on their way.

Parker and Hailey, who are a couple again, apparently, take the stragglers to IHOP. Pretty soon it's just me and Jude and Jere7my, who still hasn't found his keys.

"I don't even care anymore," he says grimly. "My mom grounds me—so what? I'm not allowed to go to all the parties I'm not invited to?"

Jude looks over at me. "Forget *Breakfast Club*. We should screen *Revenge of the Nerds*."

"What's he talking about?" Jere7my asks.

"Jude has a thing for movies that were made before we were born," I explain.

"Classics!" Jude says. "But not boring ones, like *Star Wars* or *2001* or something. In *Revenge of the Nerds*, the nerds get revenge! I mean, the title says it all."

"I'm sure it's a masterpiece," Jere7my says drily. "And I'm going to pretend I didn't hear the *Star Wars* diss."

"What are you losers talking about?"

We all look up. It's Sasha, in faded jeans and a too-big UCLA sweatshirt, carrying a box of Gold Star doughnuts. Is it even remotely necessary to say how happy I am to see her?

I didn't think so.

She reaches into a pocket and pulls out her iPhone. "Wave to the camera," she demands. "Tell it how much you love me for bringing you doughnuts."

Jude puts his hand over his heart. "I pledge my undying love for you forever if you brought me a Kevin Bacon."

"I think you're going to have to love me all the way into the afterlife, actually," Sasha says, "because I brought you two."

Jere7my stares hungrily at the box of sweets. "I am experiencing sudden yet surprisingly deep feelings of affection for you," he says.

Sasha turns to me, smiling her ravishing smile. "What about you, Theo? How much do you love me?"

Um...

38

Honestly, I have to think she knows the answer to that question. If she doesn't, maybe she's not the genius I thought she was.

"Foster pleads the Fifth," Jere7my says and grabs a chocolate doughnut.

"No, actually, I don't," I say. "I can't love you for the doughnuts, because I'm mad at you."

Sasha raises one dark eyebrow. "Why on earth?"

"You didn't dance with me," I say. And while this is true, I'm not really mad about that. I'm hurt that she pulled her vanishing act again. And also? If I said anything more right now, I'd probably confess how I feel about her, which isn't something I want to do in front of Jude and Jere7my.

She laughs. "Poor Theo. But I can remedy that, you know," she says.

She walks over to the jerry-rigged stereo and plugs in her phone, and then the melancholy, gorgeous opening chords of "Heroes" by David Bowie come through the speakers. Sasha holds out her hands for me to take, and I don't hesitate. I walk right up to her and wrap my arms around her waist. Maybe she's surprised, but then her arms circle around my shoulders.

I, I will be king, Bowie sings, *and you, you will be queen...*

I sort of feel like I'm king of the broken and she's queen of the crazy, but I don't care. I'm dancing with her as the sun climbs over the water and lights the green trees on fire. It's goofy and embarrassing and amazing, and I never want it to end.

"Where'd you go last night?" I ask softly. "Weren't you having fun? Or is 'fun' another one of those words you don't like?"

I expect her to laugh, but she doesn't. She says, "I needed some time to think."

"About what?"

"I don't know. Secrets, I guess," she says.

My body quickly goes tense, though we're still dancing,

still swaying above the pond, ignored by Jude and Jere7my, who are bent over the doughnut box like starving men.

"What kind of secrets?" I ask uneasily.

Bowie sings, *We're nothing, and nothing will help us...*

Sasha steps away from me. "Can we sit?" she asks. Holding my hand in hers, she leads us back to Jude and Jere7my.

Jude looks up, powdered sugar on his cheeks. "Is it my turn on the dance floor?" he asks. "Because I'm still busy murdering this doughnut."

"No," Sasha says, "it's your turn to film, so get out your phone. You can edit what's coming next so that it's intercut with you all saying how much you love me." She gives me a little half smile. "Not that Theo contributed to that part."

I just stare at her. I have no idea what's going on.

"Okay, are you recording?" Sasha asks Jude.

Jude nods. "*Operation Innocence: The Film,* scene seventy-something, take one," he says, and he presses Record.

Sasha takes a deep breath. "It's sort of hard to figure out how to say this. I mean, not literally, because obviously I know the necessary words and how to pronounce them. It's more like..." She stops and gazes up toward the sky like the rest of her sentence might be floating around up there. But it's not, obviously, and after a few seconds, she snaps back to attention. "The point is, these last couple of weeks have been weird and terrible, but if there's one thing that has made them less terrible, it's you guys. Okay, technically you're two things, not one. Theo and Jude, you are two humans with the power to decrease, marginally, the intensity of life's general suckage. Don't let that go to your heads; I'm not saying you're miracles of humanity or anything. But hanging around with you—sometimes by choice and sometimes definitely not—made me realize how alone I'd been before all this. The thing about books is that they don't talk back. And most of the time that's a great thing about them. But every once in a while it's nice to have a conversation. It's nice to learn things you didn't know about people, and it's good to tell them things they don't know about you." She pauses. Straightens her shoulders. "And I have something to tell you now."

I hold my breath. Her eyes, the color of the sky in winter, look directly into mine.

"I'm not innocent," she says. "I took the money."

39

I inhale sharply, and I can see the camera wavering in Jude's hand.

"I took it, and I'm not sorry," Sasha says.

"This is an unprecedented and scandalous admission from the female Homo sapiens," Jere7my chirps.

"Shut up," I hiss. I glance over at Jude, who's trying to keep the camera focused on Sasha's pale, defiant face. He's not mouthing *I told you so* at me, though obviously he was right about her. But he looks as stunned as I feel.

Nobody says anything for a few seconds, and then Jude blurts, "Why? You don't even need the money!"

She's not looking at me or the camera anymore. She's picking at her fingernails. "It was an act of protest," she says.

"Were you protesting against Arlington student consumption of sugary carbonated beverages?" Jere7my asks.

"It was a protest against that entire institution," Sasha says. "They act like it's a place of learning and understanding, but it's just a jail with geometry homework. A cinder-block monstrosity populated by teenagers dull-witted from snapchatting and adults bitter from spending the last twenty years watching their dreams slowly die, suffocated by Scantron forms, illegible algebraic equations, and plagiarized, subliterate English essays."

"Riiiiight," Jude says.

"My affection for her only grows stronger," Jere7my says under his breath.

"So what did you do with the money?" asks Jude.

"Nothing," Sasha tells him. "It's under my bed."

Jere7my blinks at her. "My experience with females is limited, so tell me, my beloved, are you all this batshit?"

Sasha ignores him. She turns to me, as if expecting me to say something. But I've got nothing. All I can think is: *She lied to us.*

She lied to us over and over and over.

"It was so stupid," she says. "It wasn't an act of protest at all in the end—I realize that. It was just petty theft."

"Well, depending on how many quarters are in the bags,"

Jere7my offers, "it could be *grand* theft. That would be approximately…"—he does a quick calculation—"twenty-five pounds of quarters."

"I don't know how much it is," Sasha says. "I never even opened the bags."

Suddenly the words are coming out of me in a flood. "How could you just pretend you were innocent? Were you just going to keep lying to us forever? Lying to *every-one*? You're such an asshole! You accused me of not find-ing out who framed you, when the fucking *money* was in your *bedroom!*"

Sasha flinches, but her expression immediately goes cool and hard. "Maybe I thought you ought to focus on someone else's problems for once. You were always so concerned about yours."

"Yeah, maybe because no one else gives a shit about them," I say.

"Says who? You have no idea. You spend so much time thinking about yourself you don't even know what's going on."

"Are you kidding?" I yell. "I think about other people— I think about *you*—the majority of my waking hours. Do you know how hard I tried to make you smile, keep you happy?"

Sasha's crying now, and she wipes the tears angrily from her face. "Well, I guess you just haven't done a very good job, Theo Foster," she says. She stands up. Kicks at the doughnut box. "And by the way, I *never* said I was innocent. You just wanted so badly to believe it, you stupid, romantic, oblivious idiot."

40

I'm lying facedown on my bed when I hear the bedroom door open. I don't roll over, because I don't give a single shit who it is. I'm not in the mood for talking.

"You missed the good part." The voice is Jude's.

I can't imagine what he's referring to. How could there be a good part to betrayal?

"All right," Jude says when he sees that I'm not moving, "you're going to act all pissed off and silent. That's cool. I get it. But I think you ought to know what happened after you stormed off."

He nudges me, and I swat his hand away.

Jude sighs. "Really?"

Still I say nothing.

"I *could* just leave you here to slowly asphyxiate in your pillow," Jude says. "But because you're my best friend, I will tell you this before you succumb to sulkiness and lack of oxygen. After you left, I kept filming, and Sasha kept talking. And I brought you the video."

I can't help it—I want to know what she had to say. I turn over.

"He lives!" Jude cries. "Theo Foster will not suffocate on my watch!" He holds out his phone.

But I can't make myself take it.

"You're being really difficult, you know." Jude puts the phone down on the bed and pats it like a pet. "So I'll just leave it here for you. But bring it by later, or else I'll go through Candy Crush withdrawal." And then he stands up, gives me a weird, awkward salute, and hurries back out.

Whatever excuses Sasha has, I tell myself that I really shouldn't care anymore. But of course, after staring at the phone for a minute, I pick it up. I can't help it. I open the video.

And there she is, bright and alive and small enough to hold in my hand. The camera is focused on her pale, lovely face—and in the background I can see myself, blurry, stalking away in fury. Sasha turns around and watches me go.

"Shit," she says. And then she doesn't say anything for a while. Doesn't even look at the camera. But Jude keeps filming, and eventually she looks up and starts to talk. "Look, everybody has secrets," she says. "We wouldn't be ourselves if we said, *out loud,* everything that we thought. We'd barely even be *people*—we'd be boundaryless amalgams of boring, basic desires with a dash or two of average, utterly familiar fears." She pauses. Gives a flicker of an embarrassed half smile. "Okay, maybe that sounds a little pretentious. I think what I'm trying to say is that it's our secrets that make us who we are, just as much as our hopes and our dreams do."

At this point Jere7my can be heard muttering skeptically offscreen. Sasha ignores him and goes on. "So I think secrets can be a good thing. And maybe they're only *not* good when they weigh on you—when you feel like your life depends on keeping them. I didn't feel bad for stealing the money. When the fact that I'd taken it was a secret between me and the anonymous world, it didn't bother me at all. But when it became a secret between me and you and Theo, then it started to weigh on me. Not the theft—the *lie.* So I decided to tell, even though it would risk our friendship. Even though I was safe, because you dopes never would've figured it out."

There's another grunting sound off camera, and Sasha raises one eyebrow. "Really, Jude?" she says. "You had your suspicions?"

207

I can hear Jude say softly, "Yeah," and Sasha smiles at him.

"I'm impressed," she says.

"It's not that I'm so smart," Jude says. "It's just that, statistically speaking, most people who are convicted of a crime are actually guilty of it."

Sasha cocks her head. "Cite your source," she says.

"Whatever," Jude says, "I always knew you were crazy."

Sasha smiles again. Then her face goes serious. "God, I thought admitting it would make me feel better. But I feel the same. Or actually, no, I feel worse. I hurt Theo, and I never wanted to do that."

"Maybe you should tell another secret," Jude says. "Maybe one wasn't enough, and there's something still weighing on you."

Sasha's eyes go bright with tears. She presses her lips together and shakes her head back and forth. "That's all I have," she whispers.

Then the video stops. I put down the phone. And I know in my heart that she's lying.

41

What am I supposed to do now? It's not like I can just call Sasha up and tell her that everything's okay, because it seems pretty clear to me that everything isn't. Not with me, and not with her.

Anyway, she hates that word. *Okay.*

I press Play again and listen to her voice, tinny and small through the phone speaker.

We wouldn't be ourselves if we said, out loud, everything that we thought.

It's crazy, but in a way, I barely even know Sasha Ellis. But then *that* fact seems crazy in a totally different way. We've spent a lot of time together since that birthday I got to spend in an expulsion hearing—shouldn't those hours add up to something?

But maybe it's impossible to really know anyone—even your friend, your crush, or your own dead father.

I sit down at my desk. I can see the letter my dad wrote me, sandwiched between the spines of two of my favorite books, just the edge of it sticking out. I touch it like I'm expecting it to burn me.

When it doesn't, I slide it out. I take a deep breath. I don't think I'm strong enough to read this.

But I guess I'm going to do it anyway.

My dear Theo,

This isn't a letter I ever thought I would have to write. But here I am, on my tenth draft no less. I hope this time I do it right, because it's very late and I am losing strength.

Being your father was the greatest joy of my life. That is what you must always remember.

When you were born colicky, I held you as you cried all night.

When you learned to walk, son, you took your first steps toward me.

When you were six, I taught you how to throw a fastball, because that's what dads are supposed to do, right? Well, you quickly broke my nose with one.

When you were eight, I woke you every summer morning before dawn so we could fish as the sun rose over our pond.

When you were twelve and we both got pneumonia, we watched movies side by side on the couch until, on day four, our DVD player spontaneously combusted. I think it objected to having to play DIE HARD for the tenth time.

When you were fifteen, you were suddenly taller than me.

When you were sixteen, you saw that I was sick. And looking you in the eye as I told you what that sickness meant was a pain deeper than I had ever experienced.

There are only so many tomorrows—that's true for all of us, whether we want to admit it or not.

Being your father was the greatest joy of my life.

I don't mind dying, Theo. What I do mind—what shatters me—is leaving you and your mother.

But nothing's working right anymore, and it is only getting worse.

I will love you forever, from wherever I'm going.

Being your father was the greatest joy of my life.

I know, I said that three times already.

That's because you truly must remember it.

All my love,
Dad

It's hard to read the end of the letter through the tears. I fold it up and I slip it into a drawer.

I sit there, for an hour or more, just wrecked. And then I wipe my face and go outside.

42

Jude's on his front lawn, his easel set up to face the street. "I've never painted en plein air before," he says as I trudge up. "It's novel and everything, but bugs keep landing in the wet paint."

When I don't say anything, he squints at me. "What's wrong?" he asks.

"I don't want to talk about it," I say. "I just want to not think for a little while."

Jude's brow furrows. "Is it Sasha?"

"No." I lie down on the warm grass near his feet. I'm trying to keep it together.

"Well, that's different." Jude peers down at me. "I get it. You want me to do the talking. You want me to distract you. Okay." He pauses. Inhales. "Here goes. My mom chewed me out about the roses, which was unsurprising, but get this: my dad was stoked. Says he's always hated roses and that he much prefers *lilies*." Jude pops the end of a paintbrush into his mouth and gazes thoughtfully at his canvas. I can feel his attention turning back to his art.

"Please keep talking," I say.

"Sorry. Hmm. Alfie humped a hole in Sex Pig and now its stuffing is coming out. A little needle and thread, though, and he'll be as good as new. Keep going?"

I nod.

"I just read an article about a guy who paints with his penis. He calls himself Pricasso. Apparently he makes bank."

I'm barely listening; I just let Jude's words wash over me. The sun feels good on my face, and the air smells like flowers. I'm trying not to think about my dad or Sasha or my ruined future.

"I heard that Hailey Page and Parker Harris aren't actually a couple again. Supposedly she's got a dick pic and is threatening to *disseminate* it—pun intended. Although that could be a lie. You really can't trust that girl."

"What did she do to you anyway?" I ask, just to keep him talking.

"I don't want to talk about it," Jude says.

"Come on, it can't be that bad. You guys were, like, ten."

"No."

"Jude, I wouldn't ask if I didn't need it, okay? Tell me a story."

Jude sighs. "Fine. It was at summer camp. You know I never liked camp—not the crafts, not the singing, not the swim lessons, *nothing*. And Hailey and her little friends knew it, and they decided to make things even worse for me. They did a lot of petty shit first—salt on my corn flakes, whatever. But the big thing was the spider." Jude kicks me lightly but resentfully in the leg. "I can't believe you're making me relive this. Anyway, they got this giant rubber spider, tied some fishing line to it, and then draped it over a rafter right above my bed. After lights out, they snuck outside and grabbed the other end of the fishing line, which was hanging out the window. So there I am, just lying in my cot, wishing I was back home in my four-hundred-thread-count sheets, and Hailey drops this *cold dark nightmare* of a spider right toward my face. I scream bloody fucking murder, because it looks big enough to eat me alive. And everybody wakes up and runs outside in their underwear, scared shitless. And they blame *me* for scaring *them*. For *their* half-naked humiliation. It was awful." Five years later, his cheeks still flush at the thought.

I can see how that could be kind of scarring. "Did she get caught?"

"Yeah, she got sent home. Served her right, shifty pig-tailed bitch."

I finally sit up. Brush the grass trimmings from my shirt. "If she's that devious, maybe she really did post the picture to my Twitter," I say.

"She said she didn't," Jude reminds me.

"Yeah, I know, and Sasha said she didn't take the quarters. So obviously we're dealing with some less than perfectly honest people."

"Are we going to have to go interview her again or something?"

"Look, I'm sorry if you're bored with the movie, Jude. I'm sorry if you don't care anymore what happens to us because you've got some great plan for yourself. *I* still care. I'm not going to stop asking questions until someone gives me a decent answer!"

Jude's shoulders slump. "I do care," he says. "And I need answers, too. For a while I thought I didn't, but I do."

I sit up. "Did something—"

"I got rejected from the summer program at Interlochen, which is basically a world-class arts camp," Jude says. His expression is dark. "They said that 'in light of my recent disciplinary action' they felt I wouldn't be a 'positive influence in their artistic community,' or some bullshit thing like that. Theo, Interlochen was a rung on the ladder. Interlochen summer program this year, then next year CalArts, then I'm off to fucking RISD or Yale. I missed my rung! What do I do now?" He kicks at his easel leg. "Shit. Another goddamn fly in the paint."

"I'm sorry about Interlochen," I say. "If it makes you feel any better, I got rejected from 7-Eleven."

"It doesn't," Jude says.

"On the bright side, though, you can use the fly," I say.

He stares at me. "Huh?"

"Call it a mixed-media piece."

Jude's face brightens ever so slightly. "Have you heard of the artist Chris Ofili? He uses, like, glitter and elephant shit in his paintings, and they're worth millions." I see him starting to smile. "You're good, Theo. 7-Eleven doesn't know what they're missing." He turns the painting toward me. "Voilà—*Bug Graveyard #1*: canvas, oil paint, fly carcass, mosquito wings."

It's an abstract swirl of color and line. It kind of looks like a six-year-old did it, but what do I know?

"Awesome," I say faintly.

I thought I was going to tell Jude about the letter from my dad. But it turns out to be impossible. I can't form the words.

I don't think it's true what Sasha said—that it's our secrets that make us who we are. It's our secrets *plus* our blind spots, our squashed hopes, and our endless small and daily failures.

43

But I can't keep up the pity party, because I've got a movie to finish. So on Monday afternoon Felix and I go to Hailey's house. (Jude claimed he had a dentist appointment, and I was nice enough to pretend to believe him even though it was Memorial Day.) I knock, and Hailey opens the door wearing a carefully ripped tank top and a miniskirt that's barely wider than a belt.

"Not you again," she says, sounding bored.

"Who is it, dear?" her mother calls. "Is it the cable company? For the last time, we are satisfied with our current provider."

"No, it's—" She looks me up and down and frowns lightly. But then she also sees the camera Felix is holding.

"I'll be back in a minute, Sharon," she calls. She shuts the door and steps out onto the porch. "She hates it when I call her by her name." A small, new smile plays across her lips. "Are you here to talk to me about Parker Harris again?"

"Sort of," I say.

"And you're filming?"

I nod. I watch her posture straighten, her eyes get brighter.

"You're not going to put this online, are you?" she asks, but playfully—like she wants me to say yes.

I don't answer, partly because I don't know. If I never figure out the truth, then there's no sense in broadcasting my failure. But if I do? Well, then I hope this'll play on the Sundance Channel. Hell, I hope it gets an Oscar nomination. Best True Crime Documentary Directed by a Delinquent Teenager—do they have a category for that?

"Earlier you said you didn't have anything to do with the posting of the picture," I say to Hailey. "Do you stand by that statement?"

She giggles. "You sound like a lawyer."

"Do you stand by your previous statement?" I ask again.

"Are you serious?" she says, no longer laughing. "What a stupid question. If I'd lied to you once, why in the world wouldn't I do it again?"

"Humor me," I say. "Did you have *anything* to do with putting the picture on my Twitter feed?"

She rolls her eyes. "I swear to God, I don't know how anyone can stand to hang out with you. This investigation of yours is sooooo boring."

This time I keep my mouth shut, and I motion for Felix to move in closer so he's got a shot just of her face. In the sudden silence, Hailey sighs. Holds up her left hand, like she's a witness being sworn in by a county court registrar. "I did not *take* the picture, and I did not *post* the picture. I do solemnly swear, so help me God, or however it goes." Then she smiles, right at the camera. "If I really wanted to humiliate Parker Harris, I'd share the dick pic I made him send me."

And when I see that gleeful smile, my heart sinks a little. Because I know she's telling the truth.

"Yeah, Jude mentioned that," I say glumly. "I guess you don't need my Twitter feed to get back at anyone."

"Where is your little sidekick, anyway?" Hailey asks.

"Licking old wounds, probably," I say. "He told me what you did to him at camp."

She dismisses this with a wave of her manicured hand. "That was six years ago."

"Well, it was really mean."

"Maybe it was," Hailey admits, "but he should get over it. It wasn't about him."

"What do you mean it wasn't about him? You scared the living shit out of him."

"I *hated* camp," Hailey says. "The food was disgusting, the lake smelled like dead fish, and no one wanted to be my partner for any of the activities. My parents wouldn't let me leave early, so I ... what's the phrase? I took matters into my own hands."

"Wait a second. You terrified Jude with a spider because you knew he'd tell on you and get you kicked out?"

She laughs. "No one had to tell on me, dummy. I admitted it right away. And like I said, it had nothing to do with Jude. It could have been anyone, as long as it would get me in trouble. Jude's bed was just closest to the window."

I don't know what to say. But Felix goes, "That is some sophisticated criminal thinking for a shorty."

Hailey shrugs. "I'm not as dumb as you think I look."

"I never said—" Felix starts.

"So they sent you home," I say.

"Yep. But don't tell my parents the truth. It's a secret."

"Hailey, I'm filming," Felix says.

"Oh, yeah." She looks at the camera. "Shit." Then she grins. "Maybe I am a little dumb."

"Well, if I can't figure out who framed me, no one's going to see this at all," I say. "Thanks for talking to us,

Hailey. Is there anything you want to say to Jude before we go? Any amends you want to make?"

Hailey thinks for a second. And then she smiles her bright cheerleader smile again. "I'm sorry, Jude," she says to the camera. "No hard feelings, okay? I had to get out of that place. You were just...what's the phrase? Oh, right: collateral damage." She shrugs, then waves and turns away.

Those phrases roll around in my head.

I had to get out of that place.

You were just collateral damage.

Suddenly I have a totally new idea about who was the Picture mastermind. And as impossible as it seems, I don't think I'm wrong.

44

Here's one question for you: Why would someone who seems to have it all *just not want it?*

And now another: What would *I* do with movie-star looks and athletic prowess and girls tripping over themselves to date me?

I don't know—it's hard to imagine a transformation that radical—but it's pretty safe to say I would *not* just throw it all away. Here I am, with barely more than nothing, and I'm still holding on to it with all my might.

So what the hell is wrong with Parker Harris, and why did he toss a metaphoric grenade into the middle of his perfect life and blow it all to pieces?

That afternoon, I grab Felix's GoPro and walk over

to the nice side of town. A few blocks away from Sasha's house, I stop in front of a big Tudor with an American flag on the lawn, window boxes full of flowers, and an oversized, overpolished SUV parked under a brand-new regulation basketball hoop. It's basically Hollywood's idea of an all-American family home. And it's where Parker Harris lives.

I kick a basketball out of my way as I walk up the driveway. Adrenaline is coursing through me. I don't know what I'm going to do or say yet, but I'm not about to let that stop me. I pound on the front door. Nothing happens. I pound again, louder this time, and after a few seconds it swings open, and Parker looms in the doorway in a Seahawks jersey.

"Yo," he says. "What are you doing here?"

"Come outside," I say. "I need to talk to you."

Like some giant Labrador, Parker follows me down the front porch steps and stands there while I set the GoPro on top of his SUV. With its wide-angle lens, it can get me and the guy I once called the Abominable Bro-man in the same shot.

Parker stuffs his fists into his pockets and shrugs and goes, "So? Dude?"

I take a deep breath. And then I pull back my right arm,

and with every ounce of strength I have in my body, I haul off and punch Parker in his chiseled jaw.

He stumbles backward in surprise, and his left hand goes to his cheek. "What the fuck?" he exclaims.

"You did it," I yell. "You posted the picture!"

Parker clenches his other hand into a fist. I think I hear a growl coming from his throat. I take a step back. I poise myself to run, because he looks like he wants to pound me into the dirt. But I can't leave yet.

"You lied to *all of us!*" I yell. And suddenly I'm so pissed I don't care if he throws a punch at me. I don't care if—

Parker swings, hard, but by some miracle I dodge it and his fist slams into the roof of the SUV. The camera wobbles, then falls onto its side.

"Fuck," he says, clutching his knuckles.

"You want to try again?" I ask. There's so much adrenaline in my blood I probably won't even feel the blow. "Come on, *bro!*"

But Parker shakes his head. "Fuck you," he says. His voice sounds tired.

"Just admit it," I say, pressing him.

"I don't know what you're talking about," Parker says.

He's not taking another swing at me, though, and that's how I know he's guilty. Everyone knows the story: If you throw two men in jail, and one of them is guilty and one of them is innocent, guess who sleeps through the night? The guilty one. Because he knows he's where he belongs.

"You *wanted* to be expelled," I accuse him. "I don't know why you wanted out, but you did. So you made the whole thing happen."

Parker watches me as I pace before him, trying to decide whether or not I want to hit him again, even if he'd finally be pissed enough to pummel me. His cheek's red now, angry looking. But he doesn't say anything. He just turns and starts walking away.

I grab the camera and hurry to catch up to him. "Don't you have anything to say? Are you going to deny it?"

Parker's shoulders are hunched and he's stalking up the street. He wants me to leave him alone, but I refuse to.

"Sasha's guilty, too. You know that, right? But at least Sasha didn't take anyone down with her when she went. At least she had the courtesy to be stupid in a way that didn't screw over anyone else."

Parker's still walking, silent and hunched, and I have to jog to keep up with him. "You have anything to say for yourself?"

"If you don't shut the fuck up," he says through gritted teeth, "I'm going to punch you back. For real this time. And it's going to hurt."

So I bite my tongue, but I keep hurrying along next to him. Up ahead, the street ends in a cul-de-sac. Beyond it there's a fence and a grassy field and, on the far side of that, the road heading out of Pinewood.

Parker stops at the fence. He leans against the top railing, and I can hear it creak in protest. "Shit," Parker mutters. "Goddammit. Fine."

"Fine what?" I demand.

Parker pushes himself off the railing again and stands in front of me. I hold the camera on him.

"I'm the reason the picture got on your Twitter account."

"I knew it," I yell. "How'd you do it?"

"*I* didn't do it. Jere-seven-my Sharp did."

No shit. "Why did—"

Parker sneers at me. "Cuz I asked nicely," he says. "No, because I paid him, dumbass, and because I'm the only jock who never pissed in his gym shoes."

"Aren't you a prince," I say.

He laughs bitterly. "Yeah," he says, "I was."

45

Even though I already guessed Parker's guilt, I'm still reeling. Apparently I didn't want to believe my own suspicions.
I exhale slowly.

But I still wish I could kick the shit out of him.

"Okay, leaving aside the Jere-seven-my question—why
in the *hell* did you do it?"

Parker kicks at a clump of unmowed grass. "Because
I felt trapped, okay? Because I hated where I was, and I
hated what I was doing."

"Oh, poor you," I say snidely. "It must be so *difficult* to
be the emperor of football."

"*You* try weight lifting two hours every day. Protein
shakes and Muscle Milk. Weigh-ins. My dad waking me

up every morning at 5 a.m. and making me run eight miles in total goddamn darkness—"

"Maybe consider yourself lucky that you still have a dad," I interrupt.

But Parker doesn't even hear me. "It wouldn't be so bad if I wanted any of it. But it's not even *my* goddamn dream. It was his."

I shake my head. "You were too much of a pussy to admit you hated it, so you got yourself kicked out? And you got me and Jude kicked out, too? Tell me, because I'm dying to know, just what's so hard about playing a *sport?*" I practically spit the word.

"You have no idea! They tracked my food and sleep—they monitored my shit schedule like it was national breaking news. They shot me full of chemicals like I was a prize-winning steer!"

"Wait—*what?*"

Parker looks around, and then, seeing no one else, he unzips his jeans and starts to pull the backside of them down.

"Whoa," I go, "I don't want—"

"Shut up," Parker hisses. He works his jeans down lower so I can see half of his left ass cheek, where the skin is puckered and red—a big, angry scar.

"What the hell?"

"It was an abscess," Parker says. "A bad reaction to pinning juice subq."

"I don't know what that means," I say.

"It means that I shot steroids into my ass, dude, and it got infected." He laughs darkly. "You don't think we got to be champions just because of our natural talents, do you?"

"But I did," I say. I can't believe what I'm hearing. What I'm seeing. "Did Coach Higgins really make you take steroids?"

Parker pulls his jeans back up. "He didn't hold a gun to my head. But, yeah, he pretty much made me. And I'm not the only one."

Suddenly this conversation is a much bigger deal than my own expulsion. And now that Parker's confessed, he won't stop talking.

"I tried other ways to get out, bro. I showed up wasted on Higgins's front porch, and he should've kicked me off the team right then. But he said I was too valuable to lose. So he made me a fucking pot of coffee and then drove me home."

"But why couldn't you talk to your *dad?*" It just doesn't make sense to me.

Parker picks up a stick and starts breaking it into pieces. "Football's his *life*. He had me throwing perfect spirals by five. He quizzed me on plays over dinner. He never cared if I did my homework—he only cared if I could analyze the weakness in a team's defenses. I *studied* that shit, man! And what good is it going to do me? I'm not good enough to go pro. I *know* that." He looks me right in the eye. He's forgotten that I'm recording him. "And maybe, deep down inside," Parker says, his voice almost breaking, "he knows that, too. But he's not letting himself believe it."

"But why does he care so much?"

"It's sick, right? He was NFL—the Seattle Seahawks. But he got hurt in the sixth game of his first season. When they didn't think he was getting better fast enough, they cut him." Parker grabs a pinecone from the ground and pitches it so far into the meadow I don't even see where it lands. "So I guess now I'm supposed to live his dream for him."

"That's a pretty good sob story," I say. "But you didn't need to take me and Jude down with you when you went."

"But the picture had to be posted—everybody had to see it—or else Higgins and my dad would've denied that anything ever happened. *Fuck*." He puts his face in his hands.

"So why didn't you put it on your Facebook page or something?" I demand.

"It had to look like someone else did it. It had to look like someone was out to get me. Because if I had an enemy,

I couldn't be accused of sabotaging myself, because I'd already tried that once, remember? This way it looked like I was the victim—not the perp."

"So you picked me. And Jude and I are just your collateral damage," I say quietly.

Parker looks at me. "The Jude thing—that was just a mistake. But, yeah. You were collateral damage." He pauses. "What are you going to do now?"

I shrug. "I don't—"

Suddenly he's diving for the GoPro, trying to yank it out of my hand. I whip my arm out of reach, my finger clutched around the tiny camera, and I don't even think. I'm up and running for my life.

Surprised, Parker stumbles, giving me a few seconds' head start. But I needed more—I can already hear him breathing hard behind me. "Hold up," he's yelling. "I just want to see it—"

I will my legs to go faster, faster. My calves are on fire, and the air sears my lungs. I hit the corner and swing right, dodging a delivery truck that clips the curb and misses me by a foot. The guy honks. Parker shouts, "Theo, hold up!"

As I swing around the other side of the truck, which is rumbling to a stop, I see my opportunity. Parker will absolutely catch me—*but only if I keep running.* I pull up short, take a deep breath, and then launch myself into the open passenger side. The driver stares at me in shock.

"What the—"

"Shhh!" I hiss, my rib cage heaving.

I press myself against the cold metal wall as Parker comes shooting around the truck and pauses in confusion. *Where'd I go?* The street is empty except for a kid riding a tricycle and his grandma walking beside him.

"Shit," Parker says. "Theo?"

Naturally I don't answer. And then Parker just starts running again, as if he thinks he can still catch me.

I laugh out loud—I can't believe it worked. I watch him get smaller and smaller, and then I step down out of the truck.

"Thanks," I say to the driver. "You basically just saved my life."

The driver shakes his head. "Kids," he mutters. He spits out his open door. "Bunch of degenerates."

46

I'm guzzling a Coke and wondering if somewhere there's a tube of Bengay for my overextended hamstrings when the back door opens and Sasha slips into the kitchen.

"Hey," she says softly, easing the door shut behind her.

She looks pale, like she hasn't slept much lately. She's wearing cutoffs, a Sleater-Kinney T-shirt, and a knitted scarf around her neck. Her tiny feet are bare.

"Hey," I say back. I'm not jumping up and down with glee to see her, but after what just happened with Parker, I don't have it in me to be mad at her anymore. She screwed up, sure, but at least she didn't bring anyone else down with her.

"Can I sit?" she asks.

"Go for it," I say.

We take chairs at opposite ends of the kitchen table. It's quiet for a minute. I watch her, wondering what she's here for, while she looks everywhere but at me: at the refrigerator covered in ancient photographs, the sink half full of dishes, and the microwave that turns frozen logs into the steaming burritos that keep me alive. Compared to her shiny marble and stainless steel kitchen, mine is something of a shithole—I realize that. But I'm not going to apologize for it.

Eventually Sasha looks me in the face. She unwinds the scarf from her neck, wads it up, and pushes it toward me. "This," she says. "I made it for you."

I suck in my breath. I remember the first night I went to her house and saw her knitting, and how it shocked me that the wild, brilliant Sasha Ellis made things out of knots and yarn.

"Is this my belated birthday present?" I ask.

"No," she says. "Birthdays are lame—why celebrate the day you were forced into being? This is an apology scarf."

It's sitting on the table between us in a dark blue puddle. It looks very soft.

"My grandma used to make prayer shawls," Sasha goes on. "With each stitch, she'd say a little prayer for the person she was making it for. This scarf is like that, except that I'm an atheist, so as I was knitting I was thinking that I was sorry I hurt you. Sorry that I lied to you."

I offer her a half smile. "Well, you're hardly the first person to lie to me. Or the last," I say. "I talked to Parker—"

Sasha waves her hand through the air like his name is a gnat she can shoo away. "Can we not talk about him for a minute? I'm not done with my explanation," she says. "I realize it's ludicrous to give someone a scarf on an eighty-degree day."

"It looks really nice." But I still don't pick it up. "It's funny because you never struck me as the knitting type," I say. "It seems like a kind of grandma thing to do."

"Knitting is a great way not to think," Sasha explains. "It's repetitive and dull, which makes it calming. And also there are absolutely no terrible consequences in knitting. For one thing, who cares if you screw up a stitch, or a row, or the entire sleeve of a wool sweater? It's just *not* a big deal. And for another, you can always fix it if you want to. You just unravel and start over. In very few other times or activities can you simply *undo your mistakes*."

She pushes the scarf closer toward me. I touch it lightly. It's impossibly soft, and I kind of can't believe she made it for me. I wonder how many hours it took, how many times she thought about being sorry for lying.

"If you put it on," she says, "that means you forgive me."

"It's hotter than an oven in this kitchen, and I just sprinted two miles, and you want me to put a scarf on?"

She nods. "Then I'll know that everything is okay."

I wait for another minute and then I pick up the scarf. "Everything isn't okay," I say. "Not yet. And anyway, you hate that word."

"But you forgive me."

I can't help but smile at her. "Yeah, I guess I do."

47

"Are you sure you want the hash?" Danny, who works the Hamburger Inn fryer, asks Jude skeptically.

"Jude," I whisper, "that's the guy who's making the food—isn't that, like, a warning flag?"

Jude ignores me. "Yes, please," he says. "I would like the hash, with a side of more hash."

"Oookay," Danny says. "If you say so."

I order a stack of pancakes, and Sasha sticks with coffee.

"So are you ready for the news?" I ask. "Jude, turn on your camera."

Jude grumbles as he does so. "I've been ready since you texted me last night. I don't know why you couldn't tell me whatever it was then."

"I wanted to tell you guys at the same time," I say. "Since we all got into this together, I thought maybe we could all get out of it together."

"Get out of it?" Jude repeats. "What do you mean?"

"I mean I know who posted the photo," I say.

Jude slams his hand on the counter. "Then spit it out!"

I take a deep breath. "Parker did, with Jere-seven-my's help."

Jude's already halfway off his stool. "I can't kick Parker's ass, but I bet I can take Jere-seven-my," he says.

I reach out and grab his arm. "Hold on," I say. "Don't you want to know why?"

Jude sits back down. "Yes. Yes, I do. Tell me."

I look over at Sasha—she doesn't look that surprised. Or maybe the better way to put it is that she looks like she's not even here. Like her thoughts are a thousand miles away.

"Earth to Sasha," I say.

She turns and blinks at me. "I'm listening," she says flatly.

"It was Parker's exit plan," I say. "He didn't like his jock life, but he was too much of a pussy to admit it."

"I don't understand at all," Jude exclaims. "What's not to like about being Parker Harris?"

Then Danny shoves the plate of hash in front of him,

and Jude looks at it in alarm. "Although who knows?" he says, pushing a fatty lump with his fork. "Maybe it's just really tough not being able to figure out what a cravat is." He snickers at his own joke.

"According to Parker, he has much bigger problems," I say. Then I explain to them how his dad was living vicariously through him. How Parker hated football but couldn't break his dad's heart by quitting. How he couldn't even get kicked off the team when he tried. "And"—I pause for effect—"he was basically forced to take steroids."

"No shit." Jude whistles under his breath. "No wonder he had that eight-pack on his stomach." He puts down his fork. "This is crazy, Theo. This is huge. The climactic ending to your movie. Like in *The Usual Suspects,* when you realize at the end that Keyser Söze was behind everything. But it's not just Parker who's the guilty one. It's his dad and the coach and maybe the rest of the team..." Jude frowns. "I guess there's kind of a lot of bad guys."

"I never suspected Parker until recently," I admit. "He always seemed too dumb to be that devious."

Jude flexes an unimpressive biceps. "Do you think you and I *together* could take him out? With an assist from Sasha? I bet she fights dirty."

"I don't think trying to kick Parker's ass is the answer," I say. "Plus I already punched him."

Jude's mouth drops open. "I would have paid top dollar to see that," he says. "Why didn't he hit you back?"

"How do you know he didn't?"

"Because we'd be having this conversation in the hospital, duh," Jude says.

Sasha still hasn't said anything. I turn to her. "What are you thinking?" I ask.

She looks down into her steaming mug. "I think this coffee is probably the worst coffee I've ever had in my entire life."

"I mean about Parker," I say.

"I get it," she says.

"What do you mean?" Jude asks.

She wraps her hands around the mug as if to warm them. "I mean that I understand your life feeling like something you can't control anymore. I understand the impulse to just blow the whole damn thing up."

"So you're not mad at him for lying? For ruining my high school career?"

"What good would being mad at him do?" she asks. "Parker's always been a self-centered oxygen thief, and nothing's going to change that."

"Well, he's going to get what's coming to him," I say. "I'm going to talk to Palmieri, and I'm going to get my name cleared. I'm going to get Jude's name cleared, too.

Maybe we'll get to go back to school for the last few days. Then we can take our exams and not fail junior year."

"What if Parker tries to deny it?" Jude says.

"He can't," I say. "I got it on camera."

"But what about the doping?" Jude asks. "I mean, if you wanted to, you could bring down the school."

I shrug. "I don't want to," I say. "But maybe Arlington is just collateral damage."

48

Palmieri's back is to the door when I stride into his office and deposit myself in the chair across from his massive desk. The pleather cushion gives a loud squeak in protest.

"I wasn't aware that I had an appointment with anyone," Palmieri says without turning around. "Tim," he calls to his assistant, "did you put someone on the books?"

Tim materializes in the doorway, shooting me an evil look. "He walked right past me, sir," he says.

Then Palmieri finally spins around and realizes just who's come to see him. His hand reaches for his big black desk phone. "You are in violation of your expulsion," he says. "You have ten seconds to justify your presence. After that, I'm calling the police."

"I didn't do it," I say. "I know you've heard me say that before, and you've never believed me. But this time I have proof." I hold up Felix's camera and glance pointedly at Tim hovering in the doorway.

"It's fine, Tim. You can close the door," Palmieri says.

"I have a recording of Parker Harris admitting that he posted the picture on my Twitter account."

I expect Palmieri to look shocked. To hold out his hand for the camera. To at *least* be ready to hear what I have to say. But instead he leans back in his pleather chair and crosses his arms. "Parker Harris? That's not possible," he says. "This is a joke."

"I'm not *joking*. I've been telling you the truth the entire time!"

Palmieri shakes his head at me, like I've disappointed him yet again, and then he picks up the phone and starts dialing. Any minute he's going to have me hauled out of here in handcuffs.

I have no choice: I press Play.

"Because I felt trapped," Parker says through the phone's tiny speakers. *"Because I hated where I was, and I hated what I was doing."*

Palmieri slowly puts the phone back in its cradle, and I stop the recording. "He wanted to get kicked off the team," I say.

Palmieri takes a deep breath and then lets it out in a long, slow exhale. He does that three more times before he speaks in a low, steady voice. "Was Parker actually the one to post the picture to your Twitter account?"

"No, he had someone else do it."

"Who? Who *else* are you trying to bring down, Mr. Foster?"

"I'm not trying to *bring anyone down!*" I yell. "I'm just trying to make sure the truth gets told."

Palmieri's eyes narrow. "What about your friend Jude? Does the recording prove his innocence?"

I pause. I hadn't even thought of that. "No...not really."

"So it helps *you*," Palmieri goes on, "but not your best friend. And it brings further trouble to Parker Harris, who has already been punished—excessively, his father argues. This could even mean criminal charges, for him and who-ever broke into your account on his behalf." Palmieri lets this sink in before he goes on. "A student whose identity I can probably guess. A boy who has excellent computer skills but very few friends. A boy who has it rough already. Am I getting warm here?"

"Are you telling me that I should just keep my mouth shut?" I ask, incredulous. "Are you saying it's better for everyone if I just pretend to be the asshole who posted a shot of shit-faced Parker and some poor girl's breasts for the whole world to see?"

"Don't think only about yourself," Palmieri says. "Think about your school. The last thing Arlington needs is another scandal. Another reason for the TV cameras to be turned on us."

Now it's my turn to take a deep breath. I let it out slow and long. "Well, Mr. Palmieri," I say, "if it's bad publicity you're worried about, you're *really* not going to like what you're about to hear." I press Play again, and I watch as he listens to Parker's explosive revelation about the football team doping.

Palmieri's perpetually tan face gets very yellow.

When it looks like he just can't stand it anymore, I hit Stop.

"God fucking damn it," he says, but softly, to himself. He stands and looks me dead in the eye. "You're worried about a stupid false expulsion when there's a potential doping scandal on the horizon? Do you have any idea what this means?" For a second it looks like he's going to punch the wall, but then he just throws up his hands. "If this gets out, it could destroy the entire school."

I keep my mouth shut. I don't want Arlington to go down in flames—but I guess I don't want a bunch of jocks walking around with injection abscesses and 'roid rage, either.

Palmieri jabs a knuckly finger at me. "If this is your idea of getting back at the administration for expelling you, you'd better figure out a different plan."

"I don't *have* a plan," I say. "I just want...justice, I guess."

"Fine. You're readmitted. The board will quietly acknowledge that the expulsions of you *and* Jude were made in error. You don't even have to show up for the rest of the week. Take your finals from home, open book. Next fall, you're seniors in good academic standing."

"That's it?"

"Yes. It's all over. Provided you keep your mouth shut. About everything."

"Keep my mouth shut? But people deserve—"

"Who's to say what anyone deserves, Foster?" Palmieri hisses, leaning forward. "Do you really deserve a public proclamation of your innocence? You did have a secret, anti-school Twitter account, let's not forget. Does Jude deserve to be back in school? I didn't hear Parker say anything about *his* lack of guilt. Does the football team and the entire school deserve to suffer because of the story of one ex-student?"

"What are you saying?" I ask. I'm completely confused.

"I'm saying what's right in the moment isn't always what's best in the end, Mr. Foster," Palmieri says. "That's something I expect you'll learn as you mature."

My surprise turns to anger. "Really? Is moral decay something I ought to look forward to when I'm old?"

Palmieri puts his big meaty hands down on the desk and grips it until his knuckles go white. "You have no idea what you're talking about, you smart-ass little twerp. I liked you. Believe it or not, I was against your expulsion. But if you can't understand that I need this handled in a responsible way, then you're not as clever as you pretend to be."

"But you can't keep it a secret," I say. "I've got it on camera."

"So you think people are automatically going to believe a bitter ex-jock?"

"We'll drug-test him. We can test the whole team."

Palmieri laughs. "First of all, *we* will do no such thing. But even if we did, most anabolics are out of the blood in a month. Other PEDs are gone in days. It's not football season now, remember? Anyone tested will read clean. There won't be any real proof."

I realize that Palmieri has a point, and my heart sinks. I stand up to go before he thinks again about calling the police.

At the door, though, I turn back around. I've realized something else.

"You don't need *real proof* to punish someone, Mr. Palmieri," I say. "You of all people should know that."

49

Back at my house, I put Felix's GoPro on a tripod and sit down across the table from it, like the camera's a friend I'm having dinner with.

"Guess what I'm eating?" I ask it. "My ten-thousandth Ana Maria's chicken burrito." I slowly rotate it in front of the lens. "Exhibit A. A miracle of food technology, the frozen burrito was invented in California in 1956, and were it not for the cheapness and deliciousness of this log of beans and processed cheese, I would have been dead a long time ago." I pause then, like I'm expecting the camera to laugh or something.

This is so pitiful. I put the burrito back on its paper plate. I'm not even really hungry; I'm just totally confused.

What now? Did I just lose my chance at clearing my record and being readmitted to school? Did I just shoot my future in its face?

I have absolutely no idea.

I turn back to the camera. "When I first thought about making this movie," I tell it, "all I cared about was proving that I was innocent. Yeah, I wanted to prove Jude was innocent, and Sasha—but if I'm honest, it was mostly about me. I guess I felt like I'd better take care of myself because no one else was doing it. No offense, Mom." I offer the camera a small smile. "And it's pretty corny, but trying to make a documentary taught me a lot. I learned about clip mics and GoPros, and about how people who wouldn't give you the time of day in real life will talk your ear off if you're carrying a camera." I pick a stray bean from the plate and pop it into my mouth. "And I learned that people lie a lot. And that nothing is uncomplicated. And that you can wish for a simple, happy ending, but it doesn't matter—you can't make life into a Disney movie." I laugh self-consciously. "How's that for a news flash? Oh, and the hero isn't dashing and handsome, and he doesn't get the girl. And the girl, by the way, is batshit anyway." I poke at my sad burrito, growing cold on its plate. "I don't think trying to make a movie made anything better. Maybe I won't fail out of school completely—I guess there's still a chance of that.

But the Property will still be sold, and my dad will still be dead." I put my face in my hands. "Shit," I say.

I hear the kitchen door open, and when I look up, I see Sasha tiptoeing into the room. She smiles at me, then wrinkles her nose. "Who were you talking to and why does it smell like baboon farts in here?"

"I was talking to the camera, and I think it's my burrito."

"Disgusting," she says.

I put my hand over it. "Don't listen to her, you're perfect."

She laughs as she sits down next to me. "A little cinema verité with your microwaved dinner, huh?"

"Whatever that means," I say.

Sasha tucks a stray dark wave of hair behind her tiny ear. "It's a French philosophy of filmmaking. We've basically been doing it this whole time, in a way. Handheld cameras, natural light, synchronous sound—"

"You lost me at French philosophy."

"Don't play dumb," Sasha says sharply.

"I'm not dumb," I say, "I'm demoralized."

"Why?" She looks surprised. "You found the guilty party. You proved yourself innocent. That's all you've been talking about for weeks! You should be ecstatic."

"It turned out to be sort of complicated," I say.

Sasha rolls her eyes. "You wanted it all wrapped up in a neat little bow? Life's complicated, Foster."

"No shit, Sherlock."

"You're calling me Sherlock? *I* never claimed to be the detective."

"You didn't have to," I counter. "You knew you were guilty."

"Touché," Sasha says.

"Palmieri isn't on our side," I say. "And Parker might deny everything anyway."

She sighs. "All right, turn off the camera. Let's get out of here."

"Why?"

"For one thing, because of the baboon fart smell. But also because I'm calling a cast and crew meeting."

"How come?"

She claps me on the shoulder. "The show must go on, Theo."

"What do you mean?"

"You're going to write your own ending," she says. "Just like you wanted."

And then she won't say anything more.

50

It's the golden hour at the Property, when the May light slants across the landscape and everything looks so soft and beautiful it hurts. We're sitting in a circle on the sun-warmed deck: Jude in a paint-splattered T-shirt, Jere7my looking zombie-ish from pulling an AP calc all-nighter, and Sasha, barefoot and wearing huge movie-star shades, as if the setting sun's still too bright for her.

Felix clips a small video camera to the railing on a gooseneck mount and looks into the viewfinder to make sure we're all in frame. "You're one motley-ass crew," he says, coming down to join us in the circle.

" 'A brain, a beauty, a jock, a rebel, and a recluse,' " Jude says.

Jere7my sniffs. "I resent your stereotyping."

"It's the tagline from *The Breakfast Club,* dork," Jude says. "Also, don't talk to me right now, because I'm seriously pissed at you." He looks around. "It sort of fits, actually. Sasha's the brain, I'm the beauty—" He yelps and rubs his arm where Sasha's just swatted it. "Ow, girl, that hurt."

"We're not here for witty banter," Sasha says. "We have something to discuss."

"Like how we're going to band together to kick Parker Harris's ass?" Jude asks. "Where is the jock anyway? Too chicken to show his face?"

"I'm right here, gonad," Parker says, coming up the deck stairs from the woods. "Had to take a whiz."

Jude shoots me a look, like *Do we try to take him?* I shake my head. This is Sasha's meeting. Let her decide what happens next.

She glances around at all of us. "In a way, we've come to the end of our story," she says. "We know who did what, and why he did it."

"Or she," I add. Okay, I don't really know the *why* Sasha took the money, but I'm not sure she does, either.

"We've got our answers," she goes on. "But sometimes the answer isn't the end of things. Sometimes you need to push on a little further because there's more to discover. A different finale."

"Cut the motivational speech. Define the optimal outcome," Jere7my says nasally.

I can see Sasha biting her tongue; I admire her for not tearing him a new one. She turns to me. "Theo, do you want to tell everyone what happened this afternoon?"

"Yeah. I went to Palmieri and I told him everything." I glance over at Parker, who jerks forward like he's going to go after me, but Sasha stops him with a single finger on his arm.

"It's not like he can expel you again," she reminds him.

"Goddamn snitch," Parker grunts.

"So what did Palmieri say?" Jude asks.

"He wanted to know if Parker had figured out what a cravat was," Jere7my says. "Everyone heard he was having trouble with that."

Sasha turns on him. "Shut up, you fungus-pale, squeaky-voiced, tube-sock-wearing deviant," she says. "You're a big part of why we're in this mess. So let Theo talk."

I guess she couldn't make her self-restraint last. Jere7my shrinks a little and mimes zipping his mouth.

I watch Parker warily as I go on. "Palmieri told me that I wouldn't fail the year—as long as I kept my mouth shut," I say. "He told me that life was about compromises, and that what's true and what's right aren't necessarily the same things." I pause. "But personally, I think that's bullshit."

Jude nods. "We can't pretend we don't know what's going on. Steroids are crazy dangerous." Then he turns to Parker. "Do they shrink your nards?" he asks, because apparently he just can't help himself.

"They turn 'em to acorns," Jere7my says. "That's why the whole football team wears bikinis in the shower."

"It's not funny," Parker says.

"He's right," I say, and I wonder if this is the first and last time I will ever agree with Parker Harris.

"So what would Palmieri do if you didn't talk?" Sasha asks.

"He sure as hell wouldn't fire Higgins," Parker says. "We've won state playoffs every year he's coached. Do you know how much bank he brings in? The football program has crazy donors, and that money gets spread around. You think the library computers got funded from those dumb bake sales the book nerds had? Think again. You're *all* sucking off the football teat."

"Ugh, thanks for that image," Jude grumbles.

"Well, we need to put a stop to it," I say. "Parker, you're the key. You were the *victim*. If I speak, will you back me up?"

Parker stares out at the pond as a family of mallards glides by. "It'll fuck up everything."

I don't blame him for his reluctance. Would I stand up if I still had anything to lose?

"You know what, Parker?" Sasha says quietly. "It's a way out. It means you don't have to admit you hate football. You just have to admit you hate steroids. Hated what they made you feel like."

"You mean like the Incredible Hulk?" Jere7my asks. "Doesn't sound that bad to me."

Parker turns to him. "Try it sometime and maybe you'll top ninety-eight pounds," he growls. "But they suck, dude. You get manic. You drink too much and you don't sleep enough. You get zits on your chest and random boner syndrome. Keep it up and you get forearms like Popeye and balls like Raisinets."

"Right! So this can be your *way out*," Sasha says again. She puts her hand on his shoulder. "And it's the right thing to do."

"Says the liar and the thief," Jere7my mutters.

Parker looks grim. "Higgins has everyone so brainwashed," he says. "It'll be just my word against his."

"But you have us," I remind him.

Parker barks a laugh. "Yeah, what are you going to do? Tweet about it? Write a letter to the editor?"

An idea is slowly forming in my mind. If it works, I think I might have the makings of a brand-new ending.

"Felix," I say, "remember what I told you when I was trying to get you to help us out?"

He shakes his head. "Nope."

"I said 'Everyone knows that if you want people on your side, you need publicity,' " I say. "And I think I know how to get it."

51

"*I don't know,*" *Jude says, looking* around nervously. "This really might be your most insane idea yet."

It's noon on Friday, and we're outside one of the high school gymnasium's emergency exits. I can hear the dull roar of the Arlington student body on the other side of the double doors, settling onto the bleachers for the end-of-year assembly.

"Where's everybody else?" Jude asks.

"Jere7my and Felix are inside, obviously," I say, "since they didn't get expelled. But Parker and Sasha will be here any moment." I pause. "I hope."

Jude bounces up and down on his toes and waves his arms around. "This is me trying to get rid of excess anxiety," he explains. "This is me trying not to think about how stupid this plan is."

"It's only stupid if it doesn't work," I say.

"What are the chances?" Jude asks.

I shrug. "Who knows? But haven't we learned to live on the edge?"

"Just don't expect me to speak," Jude says. "I'm only here for moral support."

Then I see Parker jogging over to us, untying his Chase Academy tie. "Hey, look. Here's the star of the show," I say, trying, for Jude's sake, to sound upbeat.

But Parker looks twitchy and weird—like he's having second thoughts.

"You okay?" Jude asks him warily. "Because we totally don't have to do this."

"Yes, we do," I say.

Parker shrugs. Grunts.

I don't know what that's supposed to mean, but it's not exactly confidence inspiring.

"You need to remember that we're doing the right thing," I tell him. "Thanks to you, the next generation of jocks won't have to ruin another person's life just to get kicked off the football team." Then I grin and throw a fake punch at his slab of a shoulder, pretending a certainty I don't remotely feel. "I'm kidding, bro. What I mean is, thanks to you, no other Arlington kid's going to have to shoot up human growth hormone. Seriously, Parker. You're going to help a lot of people today."

Parker clenches and unclenches his fingers while Jude and I wait nervously. Finally, he says, "Okay. Fuck it. I'm ready."

"What about Sasha?" Jude asks me.

I've been scanning the parking lot, the streets, and the sidewalk for the last ten minutes and there's been no sign of her. "I guess she misses the final scene," I say.

From inside the gymnasium comes the shriek of microphone feedback and then a reluctant hush as the assembly begins.

"Go time," I say.

Right then, the emergency doors bang open to reveal Jere7my, grinning maniacally as he motions us inside. Felix hovers right behind him, his camera trained on us.

Palmieri stands at the podium, already spouting some BS about what a great school year it was and how next year is going to be even better. And suddenly I'm almost bowled over by *nostalgia,* of all ridiculous things: for how this giant room smells—like old wood and dry dust and new sneakers—for how the sounds bounce around beneath the high white ceiling, amplifying and distorting themselves, and for all the people inside it, chattering and laughing like nothing bad's ever going to happen to them.

I think: *I used to belong here.*

Then Parker elbows me in the ribs and I snap back to reality. "Go time," he whispers.

Together we stride across the floor, heading right for the assistant principal. The kids in the bleachers see us and start whispering, and Palmieri tells them to be quiet. When they don't—when instead they get louder—he turns around.

He sees us, and his face twists into an expression of rage. He's pointing his gnarled wrestler's finger at us and shaking it, yelling something I can't understand in the din. We keep on walking until we're standing right in front of him. Then Parker hip-checks Palmieri, sending him reeling sideways, and steps behind the podium.

"Hey, guys, what's up? I'm back to make a special announcement," he says into the microphone, but everyone's still going crazy and they won't shut up. Parker holds up his hands for silence, though, and pretty quickly the room quiets. "Before I say my piece," he goes on, "first I want to introduce someone you all know—someone you haven't seen for a little while because he got kicked out, too. Everyone, please give a warm welcome to Theo Foster."

Palmieri reaches out and catches my sleeve, but I shake him off. "Hi, everybody," I say, leaning toward the mic. No one claps or anything, but they don't start booing, either.

Palmieri's grabbing at my elbow now, but Parker pulls him away. "Let the man speak," I hear him say.

I clear my throat as I scan the crowd. I can't read their faces, and I have no idea how they're going to react to what comes next.

"I know a lot of you have seen me walking around with a camera, and I've talked to some of you," I say. "I asked you to help me figure out who posted the picture that got me expelled. But none of you could help. Eventually I figured out the answer myself, and I confronted the guy who did it."

Standing beside me, Parker gives a little wave.

"Parker Harris has admitted that he posted the picture to my Twitter feed," I go on. "Parker? I think you have something to say." I hand him the mic.

Parker takes a deep breath. "Guilty," he says.

A rumbling murmur starts to build in the crowd, but Parker manages to quiet them again. Maybe it's the force of his alpha personality or maybe they're actually interested in the *truth*. As far as I can tell, that's not usually part of our high school curriculum.

"I didn't post the picture to hurt Theo," he tells the crowd. "I did it because Coach Higgins..." Parker pauses. Swallows. Grips the mic like he might be trying to strangle it. "Because Coach Higgins gave me juice." He looks around the huge room. "Steroids," he clarifies.

For one single second, you can, as the saying goes, hear a teeny, tiny pin drop. And then the entire room *erupts.* Palmieri shoves me to the side and makes a grab for the mic. Parker yanks it away, though, so he and I are the only ones who can hear Palmieri's desperate plea. "Everyone, please return to your classrooms. Teachers, will you please escort your students—"

But Parker isn't done. "Greatness doesn't come cheap! That's what Higgins used to tell us. And he's right. You've got to work hard to be good, and you've got to give it all to be great. But you know what? I did the burpees. I did the one-armed knuckle push-ups. I ran suicide sprints until I puked, okay? But I didn't want to stick needles in my ass anymore. So I bugged out."

By now the room's gone nuts. People are shouting, texting, and taking pictures. Nobody needs to bother with a secret Twitter account this time around, that's for sure.

"Anyway," Parker says. "I thought you all should know the truth. Peace out." Then he does a freaking *mic drop,* turns, and walks away.

Palmieri stands there, dumbfounded, as Parker slams open the emergency exit doors.

Following right behind him, with Jude close at my

heels, I can see a news van already pulling into the parking lot. *That* was crazy fast.

I shoot Parker a look, and he nods. Jude goes, "On your mark..."

We've had enough of cameras.

Without another word, Parker breaks left, and Jude and I rocket right, clean as a football trick play. No one follows us. We're breathless, we're sprinting, we're free.

52

Jude wants to hit the Hamburger Inn to celebrate the Higgins take-down, but I need some time to think. I have him drop me off at the Property because it's quiet. And because who knows how much longer it'll be mine.

And is celebration really called for anyway? Maybe we'll get a drug-pushing coach fired, but we didn't get ourselves back into school. Our futures are still in question, and I'm starting to get really sick of the uncertainty.

"Do you think these are a good addition to the collection?"

I whirl around, and there's Sasha, holding up a string of lights shaped like Japanese beckoning cats.

"Jesus, you scared me," I say. "Where'd you come from?"

She smiles, dazzlingly, and suddenly I start to feel more optimistic. If Sasha Ellis is going to be part of my future, how bad can it be?

"I've been here all afternoon. You walked right past my car."

I look where she's pointing, and there it is, tucked in between two huge rhododendron bushes. "You camou-flaged it," I say defensively.

Shrugging, she says, "Surprise!"

"Where were you earlier? I thought you were coming to school. I thought you wanted to be a part of the grand finale."

"You know me, Theo," she says, winding the cat lights around the deck railing. "I'm not big on public displays of disaffection."

"Very funny."

"Felix texted me the assembly video," she says. "It's amazing. After you left, there was basically a riot. Everyone storming the podium, Palmieri running off with his tail between his legs... God, what an ending that'll make."

"Sure, if we ever put the thing together."

Sasha looks surprised. "Why wouldn't you?"

"I guess I don't know what the point is now. The truth's

out, but it's not going to change anything. Not for me, anyway. No one cares about the picture. They've moved on to what even *I* can admit is a larger problem."

She puts her hand on mine. "Poor Theo," she says. "Justice is never served."

I slide my hand away. "Don't patronize me."

"I'm not," she insists. "I'm being sympathetic. I just... Oh, God, I don't even know what I'm trying to say." She looks away, then back at me. "Can we go out in the boat?"

The rowboat leans against a tree, its hull still littered with cups from the Convict Prom. "Okay," I say. I make a halfhearted attempt to clean them out, then flip the boat over and shove it into the water. I tow it alongside the dock, then climb in and fit the oars into their locks. "All aboard!"

Sasha steps carefully into the prow; the boat wobbles and she gives a little yelp. When she's sitting down, I push off, and we glide through the water toward the center of the pond.

"We're floating!" she says, sounding happy as a little kid.

"Yep. It's all about Archimedes' principle."

"Whatever that is," she says.

I can't help a small smile. "I don't need to explain my references to you, do I?"

"Nope." She pushes playfully at my knee.

And I start to think about next year, when we're both back at Arlington, however we get there. And how maybe on the first day of school I'll see Sasha, reading in a corner of the cafeteria at lunchtime. And I'll go sit beside her, and she'll put down whatever work of classic literature she's reading and start happily talking to *me*, Theo Foster. Because we're friends.

Or maybe even more than that.

The thought of this makes me embarrassingly happy.

"Why are you super smiley all of a sudden?" Sasha asks. "Is it because you single-handedly ruined a championship football team? I mean, really, not many seventeen-year-olds can claim that."

I don't think I can tell her the truth—not yet. "Yeah, just when I was convinced my life would be a tiny, meaningless blip in the vast morass that is human existence, I saved a bunch of adolescent jocks from 'roid rage and raisin balls."

Sasha laughs. "See? You just have to look on the bright side. But seriously—are you still bummed about school? Would you go back now if Palmieri said you could?"

"Of course. Wouldn't you?"

She scoffs. "And once again rub shoulders with small-town half-wits so shortsighted they think a good goal for the future is hitting Pizza Hut on Saturday? Please."

"You're so mean," I blurt. "I might be in love with you."

Oh, God—did I just say that?

She stares at me with those big, glacial eyes. "What?"

My cheeks go hot. I can't possibly say it again; I didn't mean to say it the first time. So instead I lean toward her, almost helplessly, like she's a magnet pulling me in. The boat rocks, and we both grab on to the sides to steady ourselves. She leans forward, too, and our mouths just sort of...bump together. It's almost like it's an accident, but it wasn't—not for me, anyway. And suddenly here we are, kissing. Sasha's mouth is soft and warm, and it opens to mine. I'm going to die of how good this feels. I let go of the boat with one hand, and I twist my fingers into her dark hair, hot and silky in the sun. She makes a tiny sound, a breath or a moan, and then she pulls away.

"Theo—"

"I'm so sorry," I say. Then I stop. "No, I'm not. I really like you or I love you or something in between those things, and it's been this way forever and you *have* to have figured that out by now, right?"

Sasha looks down at her hands.

"What's wrong?" I ask.

"I'm sorry. I can't do this," she says.

"Do what? Sit in a boat?" My voice is getting higher,

more desperate. "Kiss me? Have a meaningful human connection?"

She shakes her head without looking up. "I need you to take me back to shore," she says. "And then I need you to come with me to my house. There's something you have to know."

53

Sasha doesn't say a word on the whole drive to her house on the nice side of town. When she pulls into her driveway, I think she's finally going to say something. But instead she just sits there, her hands on the steering wheel and her eyes staring blankly, straight ahead.

"Are we—" I begin, but she interrupts me.

She says, "And now I need you to come inside."

"All right, I can do that," I say, trying to sound upbeat, like nothing's changed since we were in the boat. It has, of course: the mood's turned strange. But at the same time, I'm still thinking about our kiss—the surprise and the rightness of it. I felt it in basically every cell of my body, and I can still feel its echoes now.

What had it felt like to her? Was she thinking of it, too?

Opening her front door, Sasha inhales deeply and says, "Okay, here we go."

It's like it's the house of a stranger that she's entering for the first time.

Inside it's dark and cool. Sasha slips off her shoes and so I take mine off, too, and then we walk down the hallway into a cavernous living room painted a deep forest green. There are big leather chairs and floor-to-ceiling shelves of books, and unlike every other living room in Pinewood, there's no huge flat-screen TV. Instead there's a whole shelf of Gabriel Garcia Marquez, and another one of Hemingway, the spines covered in plastic like they're first editions, which they probably are.

Sasha has no patience for my obvious admiration. "I need you to come upstairs," she says.

In any other moment I'd be ecstatic—*I'm being invited deep into the dwelling of the eternally mysterious Sasha Ellis.* But there's something seriously *off* about this. There's a tight, nervous edge to the way she's holding herself, almost as if she's trying to shrink into someone even smaller. She won't look me in the eye.

We go up the dark wooden steps, and Sasha stops in the hallway. She's still not talking, and the silence is unnerving.

"Are you going to admit to me that you stole something

else? Besides my heart, I mean." I make a stupid, hideously goofy face in the hopes of breaking the tension, but it doesn't even come close to working.

"That joke is beneath you," Sasha says.

"I know," I say.

She looks so small and sad now I don't know what to do. "I'm sorry I kissed you," I blurt.

She shakes her head. "It's not that," she says.

We're standing outside a bright, airy room. There are a million books here, too, but they aren't on shelves: they're on the bed, the floor, and piled in towering stacks on the desk.

"Yours?" I ask.

She nods. "Go in if you want," she says.

"Do you want me to?"

She shrugs.

And so I walk in. The faintest flowery smell hangs in the air—of incense, maybe, or perfume. Sasha's bed is made, and her clothes have been hung carefully in the closet. The only visible mess is the books.

I pick up a book of poems by Theodore Roethke. "This is the guy your dad was quoting, isn't it?"

" 'I know the purity of pure despair, / My shadow pinned against a sweating wall,' " Sasha recites. Her voice sounds wooden.

And why does every line she quotes have the word *despair* or *hell* in it?

I set the book down again. "Sasha, what's wrong?"

"I need you to see another room."

And so I follow her down the hall again. This room is smaller and barer, with only a double bed and a rocking chair. Sunlight flickering through trees makes shifting patterns on the pale yellow walls.

"This is it," she says, stopping at the doorway. She's not looking at me—she's just staring straight ahead.

"What do you mean?" I ask. "What is it?"

She shakes her head, and then she starts sobbing.

54

I reach out and take her small, cool arm. "Sasha, what's wrong? Here, come sit down." I try to pull her toward the rocking chair inside the room, but she shakes her head sharply.

"No, not in there!"

"Okay," I say, "let's go back to your room, then."

Mutely she follows me, wiping the tears from her eyes even as they keep on falling. I sit at the foot of the bed, and she sinks down next to me.

"What is it?" I ask.

She shakes her head. "Hang on," she says, sniffling. "I have to turn off these fucking faucets. I have to..." She takes a shuddering breath. "I have to calm down."

And so I wait quietly until she's no longer crying, until she's looking at me with swollen eyes but a steely, determined gaze.

"I have something to tell you that is going to horrify you," she finally says.

"Sasha, nothing you could—"

She cuts me off. "Don't say it," she says. "You'll find that it's not true. And you're a lot of things, Theo, but you're not a liar."

"Okay," I say. "I'm not going to say anything more. I'm here. I'm listening."

Sasha turns her tear-streaked face toward the window. "If I'm going to say this, I'm not going to be able to look at you. Okay? Okay." She takes another deep, trembling breath.

I wait.

And she begins.

"It started in ninth grade, my first year in Pinewood. I'd broken up with Parker, because although he was extremely hot—sorry, Theo, it's an objective fact—we didn't have a single thing to say to each other. And my dad hated him, even more than he hates you."

"He hates me?" I ask.

"He hates everyone who wants to spend time with me. 'Oh, Sasha, what *is* the name of that giant slab of flesh who calls you?' he used to ask. 'Cretin Harris, is that it? I really don't think you ought to see him again.' His scorn made everything worse—and, well, Parker *was* kind of a cretin. So here I am, the new kid in this crappy town, and suddenly I'm totally alone. It was awful. No one was nice at all, and my dad was basically the only person who really wanted to talk to me." She takes a deep breath. "And he was a good talker. He'd seen every movie, he'd read every book, and he wanted to tell me all about them. He said he could teach me more than high school ever could, because 'the best Arlington can do is train adolescent barbarians to curb their basest urges.' Seriously, he was such a snob. But he was funny and charming—to me, anyway. He knew all about modern art and classical poetry and film noir, and he even listened to good music, like Sonic Youth and Miles Davis and Gram Parsons and Emmy Lou Harris." She pauses. "I'm trying to tell you the okay parts first, I guess. I'm working up to the part that matters."

"Okay," I whisper. I can't think ahead—I can only listen.

"Remember that we hardly even knew each other back then—it had been so long since we'd spent any real time together. And he was so interested in me! He wasn't like my mom, who'd come home at midnight if she bothered coming at all. He was always in the kitchen by five, and he'd cook a nice dinner, and he'd ask me about my day. No one had ever paid that much attention to me, Theo, and I loved it. I was the center of his world, and he was the center of mine." Her hands twist in her lap. She hesitates before going on. "Now comes the harder part."

I inhale. "Sasha—" But it's like I'm not even here anymore. She keeps talking.

"We were in the kitchen—we'd both gotten up in the middle of the night for some reason. He made me a mug of tea, and he poured himself a whiskey. And we were standing there, and suddenly he pressed me up against the refrigerator and he kissed me. I was so shocked—I didn't know what to do. And then he told me how much he loved me. He said that he couldn't believe he'd survived life without me. He said that he hadn't even known how hollow he'd been, but that being with me had made him whole. We were meant to be together, he said." She swallows. A tear slides down her cheek. "But he didn't mean like father and daughter. He meant it in a different way."

I can't believe what I'm hearing, and I have no idea what I'm supposed to say.

Still staring out the window, Sasha goes on. " 'We don't have to be like everybody else,' he'd say. 'We don't have to accept their judgments or their self-serving so-called morals. Attitudes change. Greek nobles used to kidnap young boys, take them into the forest, and rape them, and no one had any problem with that. A German ethics panel just argued that *consanguineous lovemaking'*—that's what he called it—'shouldn't be illegal.' He was so persuasive. He could argue any point in the world and you'd believe him—he could convince you the sky was orange and the grass was black. And when I resisted, he'd say, 'Darling, I love you. I need you. I don't know how I'd go on without you.' And the thing is, in some ways I felt the same about him. I'd already been basically abandoned by my mom. I couldn't have him leave me, too. And I was afraid he would if I didn't do what he wanted."

"So did you..." My throat constricts and I can't finish the sentence. Can't say the words *have sex with your father.*

But Sasha knows what I'm asking. And she nods. "I showed you the room," she says quietly. "That's where it happens."

I feel like I'm going to throw up. "Why are you telling me this?" I whisper.

"I'm telling you because now I want it to end. I can't do it, Theo. I can't take it anymore. I feel like I'm going insane. I *am* going insane. But you don't understand him. He's...he's so strong. I can't—this thing is like a speeding train, and I don't know how to stop it." She turns to me now, and her eyes search my face. I'm sure she can see what I'm trying and failing to hide—shock, rage, disgust.

I can't be here any longer. I stand up.

"Theo?" she says.

But I can't answer. All I can do is run.

Reeling, half blind with revulsion, I manage to stumble my way outside. The sun's like a punch in the gut, and suddenly I'm bending over, dry-heaving on Sasha's front lawn.

When I'm done with that, I start running home.

55

Our minivan's actually in the driveway for once, but I don't call to my mom to let her know I'm here—I just grab the keys from their hook and run back outside.

"Theo?" Her voice comes through the screen door. "Is that you?"

I put the car into reverse. "Gotta go," I yell.

She calls out something else, but I don't know what it is and I don't care, either. I'm already backing into the street.

I head east toward the edge of town. Past the Matheson's shopping center and the hideous corporate office park, the speedometer ticks a few degrees right of 75 and stays there—that's all the power the old Honda's got.

The windows are down and the air rushes into my face,

and I wish I could keep on driving forever. I wish the radio worked so I could drown out Sasha's words. I wish most of all that I could go back in time and somehow make the last year simply *not happen.*

I can't believe what life has done to me—or what life has done to her.

Now, by some miracle pushing 80, I shoot by a van that says DANIELLE'S DOGGIE DAYCARE, and the driver—Danielle, presumably—gives me the finger. So she doesn't like being passed on a double yellow? Whatever. I flip her off right back. *Fuck you and your little dogs, too.*

I can't tell if speeding's making me feel better or worse. My heart and head are both pounding. Sasha and her *father.* What in the hell is *wrong* with the world? How could a man *do* that?

I see a sign for the highway that's a couple of miles up the road. Once you're on that, it's just two hours to the city. If I go there, I won't know a soul, and no one will know me, and maybe I won't feel so much like stabbing knives into my eyes. Or finding Matthew Ellis and somehow running him over with my mom's Honda.

I press even harder on the accelerator. The minivan shudders, strains. The engine screams. And then twirling red-and-blue lights appear in my rearview mirror.

I pull over to the side of the road and slam my fist to the

dashboard. "Shitpissfuckdamn," I yell, which is what my dad used to say.

The squad car glides to a stop behind the van, and a bowlegged officer walks up to my window and bends down to look in.

"You realize why I pulled you over today?" the cop asks. Then he lifts his knockoff Ray-Bans and peers into my face. "Well, what do you know. You're Theo Foster, aren't you?"

Jesus, I think, *he knows who I am from seeing my face all over the news.* Could today get any *single shred* worse?

I nod. "Yes, sir."

Now he's leaning his elbows on the door. "You've had a rough time of it lately, haven't you?" he asks.

The sympathy in his voice is not at all what I was expecting.

"Yes, sir," I say again.

"I understand. I knew your dad," he says. "We used to play racquetball together at the rec center."

"You did?" I squint at him. I don't think I've ever seen him before.

"For two years, son. He had a wicked backhand and a killer pinch shot," the cop says. "What a terrible thing to happen to him. I'm so sorry."

But I'm so wrecked I can't even accept this stranger's

kindness. The world is full of horrors I'm only beginning to understand. "He did it to *himself,* remember?" I ask sharply. "It's not like he got diagnosed with a goddamn bullet in his brain stem."

The cop's face crumples. "Oh, son, he got delivered a death sentence just the same. He couldn't..." He shakes his head. He looks almost overcome. "It was too awful. I might've done the same thing in his place. I thought about that a lot. There just was no good choice."

But I'm not in the mood for thinking about my dad, because the more I think about him, the more shattered I feel. Maybe there was no good outcome, but there *was* a good choice.

It just wasn't the one that he made.

"Are you going to give me a ticket?" I ask through gritted teeth.

The cop shakes his head. "Not today. But I don't want to see you zipping down the road like this again, Theo Foster. There's a big curve before you hit the interstate, and I've pulled more than my share of kids out of mangled Chevys because of it." He pats the roof of my mom's old beater. "Now you turn around and go back home. Give my best to your mother. Tell her Officer Todd Tucker is thinking of her."

He stands there on the side of the road, watching as I drive back the way I came.

What am I supposed to do now?

I grip the steering wheel. *Hell is empty, and all the demons are here*—isn't that what Sasha said?

I think about her dad—an abuser. And mine—a suicide.

Are we, too, a couple of disasters in the making?

I really hope not.

I squeeze my eyes shut, count to five, and then open them again. I'm still on the road. It stretches out straight in front of me. It doesn't care which way I go.

But I realize that I do.

You gotta keep yourself between the ditches, son, my dad said when he was teaching me to drive. *Sometimes you gotta pay attention to where you* don't *want to be.*

Sometimes when I think about my dad, I can't help wondering if there was one final millisecond, as the bullet tore through his brain, when he regretted his choice.

For his sake, I hope not. A person can make amends for a vast array of fuckups. But he can't do it from inside a coffin.

I take a deep breath. I'm alive. Sasha's alive.

We're just going to have to take it from here.

56

I turn down the gravel road to the Property. The wild sweet peas are fading a little, but the daisies have begun to bloom, and the field's a riot of pink and white.

As I come around the bend, I see Sasha's car parked by the rhododendrons—not hidden this time. And then I see Sasha herself, sitting on the edge of the deck, waiting for me. I guess she knew I'd come here, the way I knew she'd be here, too.

She stands as I approach and brushes the shiny hair away from her pale face. She's not crying. Her eyes are clear and fierce. She says, "You can't do that to me, Theo. I won't stand for it."

I take her into my arms and pull her to my chest. I feel

her sharp shoulder blades, her fast-beating heart. How could anyone ever hurt her?

"I know," I say, my throat constricting in pain. "I'm sorry for how I acted. And I'm so sorry for what happened to you. I didn't know what to do or what to think, and I freaked out. So I ran. I know, it was terrible of me." I take a step back and meet her gaze. "But I'm here now, and I'm going to help you," I say.

"How?" she asks. There's no challenge to her voice. It's almost like she's hopeful.

And I realize I don't know the right answer to that question. What *do* I do? Do I confront her father? Do I call the police? Do I put her in the car and drive us both away, hoping that Officer Tucker doesn't catch me this time?

There's only one thing I'm sure of right now. "What I said in the boat—I still mean it," I say. I take her hands in mine.

"Do you really, though?" Sasha asks. "Didn't you just realize that you barely even know me? How can you love someone with so many secrets?"

"I don't know," I cry. "I'm not doing it on purpose!"

Sasha gives a small, desperate laugh. "Love's just an accident, huh? That makes perfect sense to me. Well, I guess neither of us knows what the hell we're doing, or why the hell we're doing it. It's like we're both just sitting on top of moving trains, and the world's rushing past us, and we don't know how to make it stop."

"The difference is that I don't want to stop," I say. "I love you, Sasha Ellis, and I like it that way. But you—your train is a different goddamn story."

Then I let go of her hands and I start walking toward the shed. This talk of moving trains has given me an idea. Admittedly, a crazy one.

"Have you seen any YouTube stunt videos lately?" I call over my shoulder.

"What does *that* have to do with anything?"

"Life advice," I say cryptically. "Having to do with objects in motion."

"I have no idea what you're talking about."

"You're not supposed to yet," I say. I wheel the ancient dirt bike out of its dusty shed. My mom had insisted I take it back to the Property since it wasn't road safe. "What you need is a demonstration."

I straddle the bike. Choke on, carburetor throttle open. Clutch in. I slam down on the kick start, and the bike rumbles to life.

"What are you doing?" Sasha calls over the sound of the motor.

I lurch forward, then shift into second. I don't want to be going too fast, but too slow won't do either.

In case anyone is wondering, barging into the assembly wasn't my most insane idea ever—this is.

The bike bumps over the grass. I pick up speed and the motor whines in protest. Then I hit a tree root that nearly unseats me. I grip the handlebars harder. My heart is pounding.

I can't believe I'm about to do this.

I'm trying to save Sasha, but I might destroy myself.

Oh, well.

I lean forward. I lift myself off the saddle a little. My legs are tense, knees bent, and my grip is tight. I'm heading straight for the woods, where there is no path. Where there's nothing but trees.

"Theo!" Sasha yells.

I cut between two saplings, spin around a lilac. And then a giant blue spruce looms in front of me. I bear down on it. I pull the throttle back just a bit more. Three seconds to impact.

At the very last moment, right before the tree and I meet, I thrust my legs up and over the bike. I'm suspended in the air...

And then I come crashing down. I hit the ground hard, the wind slammed right out of me. I go fetal, gasping, as the world goes blurry and then pops back into focus.

The bike keeps on going, careening into the low, sweeping branches of the tree and then hitting the trunk itself. There's the sound of crunching metal. The bike tips over and crashes to the ground. The motor dies. And then there's silence.

Sasha comes running to where I'm lying on the ground. I'm clutching my knee, which is on fire with pain.

"What in the hell?" She's practically screaming into my face. "Are you okay? What were you thinking?"

I smile up at her, dizzy with pain and exhilaration. "You were talking about a moving train, weren't you? Well that, Sasha Ellis, is a very clear and practical demonstration of how you get off one."

She stares at me in wonder and disbelief.

"Yes, it will hurt you," I say. "Possibly it will hurt a lot. But on the bright side, you'll finally be *off*."

Sasha falls to the ground and her head drops to my chest. "I love you, too, you stupid, romantic, deranged idiot," she whispers.

The End

EPILOGUE

But of course, that wasn't really the end. And it couldn't be, because we weren't a couple of actors in a dumb teen movie. We were two people trying to figure out how to live our lives in a summer when it felt like the world (or at least a good-sized chunk of it) had turned against us.

"You want a refill?" Danny asks, holding up a carafe.

I shake my head. "No, thanks," I say.

It's not that the coffee's terrible. The Hamburger Inn's made a few changes recently, and their brew no longer tastes like hot battery acid with a dash of nuclear waste. The problem is that I've had five cups of it, and my pulse is running double time.

Jude says, "I could have a refill on the hash, though."

That hasn't gotten any better, but Jude loves it anyway.

Jere7my looks at the meaty lump skeptically. "Undoubtedly that is the nutritional version of malware," he says. "It looks innocent enough, but when it enters the processing system—" He clutches his guts, mimes having massive diarrhea. "Like the Galaxy Note 7, you just explode. Amirite?"

"As a matter of fact, you are not," Jude says primly.

"If he wants to spend the first day of senior year locked in a bathroom stall, it's not our problem," I say to Jere7my. "But come on, you guys. We're going to be late."

Jude throws down a twenty for our breakfasts. He sold a painting last month and he's been playing Mr. Moneybags since. "And that's the last of it," he informs us. "Time to get my hustle back on."

We grab our backpacks and hurry the six blocks to school, where Jude and I have been returned to our former academic standing. Jude's even our mascot again, although I doubt the Fighting Tigers are going to enjoy another undefeated football season.

As for me, I'm going to try to keep a low profile. No Twitter, no nagging editorials. Palmieri resents me because he owes me, so I'm going to work on not aggravating him too much.

When the powers that be started asking around about the use of steroids, I kept my mouth shut. I never mentioned that Palmieri knew about the doping before Parker's surprise speech. Why ruin another career? Coach Higgins deserved to be fired, but—as much as I hate to admit it—I don't think Palmieri did.

I believe he would have done the right thing. We just made him do it faster.

"Slow down, you guys," Jere7my whines, struggling to keep up with us.

Jere7my's basically our friend now, although sometimes I have mixed feelings about it. He's taken to calling me Crusher, after a character from *Star Trek: The Next Generation*. I've never seen the show, but somehow I'm pretty sure it's not a compliment.

Parker stayed on at Chase, our region's number one producer of rich lacrosse bros with severe resting douche face. Weirdly, I sort of miss him.

Felix and I spent the summer editing all our footage, and we came up with a sixty-minute documentary that isn't even terrible. Maybe someday it'll come to a YouTube channel near you.

And as for Sasha, the person whose fate I worried about most (yes, by this time, I cared about hers even more than my own), she left town not long after my motorcycle "accident." Things got ugly, but she figured out how to get off her moving train. She told a teacher, who phoned the Pinewood police. Professor Ellis was quickly arrested and charged with incest and statutory rape; as far as I know, he's still in jail, awaiting trial. I try not to think of him too much or what he did to his brilliant, beautiful daughter. I try to look forward rather than back.

Sasha's trying her best to do the same. After spending the summer in DC with a cousin, she got herself a scholarship to boarding school. Her application essay, she informed me, was a profile of Spanish anarchists who see stealing as a valid political protest against hyper-consumerism. She donated her stolen quarters, plus all the money she'd swiped from her dad's wallet over years, to an organization that offers support to victims of sexual abuse.

"I'm working through things," Sasha told me via video message. Guess she's really embraced the "truthful cinema" philosophy. "Slowly and painfully. I go to a lot of therapy. I've been writing. And taking jujitsu. And I like to recite that Philip Larkin poem—you know the one. 'This Be the Verse.' It's unexpectedly comforting." Her smile is both terrible and hopeful.

I didn't know the poem, of course, but I didn't ask her to explain her reference to me.

Later, I looked it up.

They fuck you up, your mum and dad.
They may not mean to, but they do.
They fill you with the faults they had
And add some extra, just for you.

That's the first verse. And I wouldn't call it an uplifting poem, that's for sure. But I guess we should all take comfort where we find it.

I miss Sasha terribly: her razor tongue; her arctic eyes; her manic, unpredictable energy. I really did love her.

Probably I still do.

"Dude!" Jude says, waving his hand in front of my face. "You're literally about to walk into traffic."

I snap back into myself. "Sorry."

"Don't apologize to me," he says. "Just watch where you're freaking going, okay?"

I smile at him. "I know where I'm going," I say. "Finally."

And together we open the doors to Arlington High School, Home of the Fighting Tigers, where our futures—whatever glory or mess they'll be—await us.

JAMES PATTERSON received the Literarian Award for Outstanding Service to the American Literary Community at the 2015 National Book Awards. He holds the Guinness World Record for the most #1 *New York Times* bestsellers, including *Confessions of a Murder Suspect* and the Maximum Ride series, and his books have sold more than 350 million copies worldwide. A tireless champion of the power of books and reading, Patterson created a children's book imprint, JIMMY Patterson, whose mission is simple: "We want every kid who finishes a JIMMY Book to say, 'PLEASE GIVE ME ANOTHER BOOK.'" He has donated more than one million books to students and soldiers and funds over four hundred Teacher Education Scholarships at twenty-four colleges and universities. He has also donated millions to independent bookstores and school libraries. Patterson invests proceeds from the sales of JIMMY Patterson Books in pro-reading initiatives.

EMILY RAYMOND collaborated with James Patterson on *First Love* and *The Lost,* and is the ghostwriter of six young adult novels, one of which was a #1 *New York Times* bestseller. She lives with her family in Portland, Oregon.